MONSTER
ISLAND

Justin Richards

Non-fiction section by Christopher Edge

www.pearsonschoolsandfecolleges.co.uk

✓ Free online support
✓ Useful weblinks
✓ 24 hour online ordering

0845 630 33 33

Heinemann

Part of Pearson

Heinemann is an imprint of Pearson Education Limited, Edinburgh Gate, Harlow, Essex, CM20 2JE.

www.pearsonschoolsandfecolleges.co.uk

Heinemann is a registered trademark of Pearson Education Limited

Text © Justin Richards 2011
Non-fiction text © Christopher Edge
Typeset by Kamae Design
Cover design by Craft Design
Cover photo © Igorsky/Shutterstock

The rights of Justin Richards and Christopher Edge to be identified as authors of this work have been asserted by them in accordance with the Copyright, Designs and Patents Act 1988.

First published 2011

14 13 12 11 10
10 9 8 7 6 5 4 3 2 1

British Library Cataloguing in Publication Data

A catalogue record for this book is available from the British Library

ISBN 978 0 435 04597 5

Copyright notice

Printed at Henry Ling, UK

Acknowledgements

We would like to thank the following schools and students for their invaluable help in the development and trialling of this book:

Royal Manor School, Portland

Adam Clark, Ashley Friend, Karl Jolliffe, Ayrton McCusker, Brandan Plackett, Lawrence Teague-Forder.

Queensbridge School, Birmingham

Farhan Akmal, Farees Almatari, Junaid Asif, Chloe Bartlett, Shane Bevan, Tyler Blair-Thompson, Shahid Farooq, Danial Hussain, Umayr Hussain, Arbaz Mohammed Khan, Kadeem Khan, Umer Khan, Ihtishaam Majid, Arslan Mehmood, Aqila Patterson, Sophie Pinnegar, Aaron Reatus, Jamie-Lee Smith, Roche Smith, Abdallah Suleiman, Imran Uddin, Saqib Ul-Hassan, Chulothe Urooj, Keiran Von-Breen, Nikolas Watkins, Oliver Watkins, Grace Williams, Raakib Zaman.

For Alex and Zach – soon to be monster readers!

Contents

Non-fiction:

Prologue

If Dom opened his eyes, he was dead. The world was dark, but he could see flashes of light through his eyelids. Dom knew that if he opened his eyes, everything would be brilliant white. White walls, white floor, white lights. White-coated figures wheeling the trolley on which Dom lay. If he opened his eyes, he'd be staring at the ceiling – and that was white as well. Clinical and sterile, like you'd expect a hospital to be.

He had to time it right. He tried to stay calm and relaxed. Tried not to breathe too heavily or seem nervous. Tried not to frown with worry or swallow in fear. He'd only have a moment, and he would never get another chance. Never.

The metal of the handcuff was cold round his wrist. It would take them only a moment to uncuff him from the trolley, lift him into the bed and cuff him to the side rail. But that moment would be enough. His last chance.

Dom felt weak and sick from the anaesthetic. There were vague shapes in the darkness as he struggled to keep his eyes closed. He thought of his mum – he hadn't seen her since they'd sent him to the home. The other children from the group – Katie laughing and Carlo smiling – all of them looking forward to the tour. Not knowing what was about to happen to them. Dom wondered if they were even still alive.

There was a gentle bump. Dom recognised the change in flooring as the trolley was wheeled into the bedroom. He wondered how many white coats there were. If he was lucky, it was just the woman with the dark hair and green eyes and maybe the short man with greasy hair. If he was unlucky, the brutish fair-haired man would be there – tall and broad and grinning at the pain. The last thing Dom had seen before he passed out this time was the fair-haired man's unpleasant smile. He didn't want to see it again. Not when he opened his eyes, not ever.

There was a metallic rattle of keys. The cold metal on his wrist dropped away, though he could still feel the memory of its impression. Two sets of hands lifted him gently. It seemed easy – he'd lost so much weight since he'd been here. But right now he couldn't sense the uncaring roughness of the fair-haired man. He might be lucky.

In his mind's eye, Dom could see the room. He could see the pale plastic curtains hanging from a rail set in the ceiling round the bed. He could see himself being lowered on to the bed. He could see the cabinet beside the bed, on it a plastic water jug and beaker. He could feel the mattress hard against his back. Then he heard the clank of the side rail being lifted back into position. Next they would put the handcuffs back on. It was now or never.

'The kid's dead to the world,' a voice said. A man's voice – was it the fair-haired man? Dom felt his heart skip a beat.

'Still need to restrain him,' a woman answered. A warm hand lifted his wrist.

Now or never.

Dom's eyes snapped open. For a moment, he was dazzled by the bright white of it all. The only respite was the dark splash of the woman's hair. The red of her lips. The green of her eyes, like a cat's. She was looking right at him. She opened her mouth to say something – maybe to reassure him that everything was all right.

But it wasn't all right. It hadn't been all right since he got here.

Dom launched himself off the bed, drawing on every last bit of energy he had left. He knocked sideways into the woman. Handcuffs clattered to the floor. The woman sprawled backwards. She grabbed at the plastic curtain that hung round the bed, snapping it from its rail as she fell.

The man was moving from the other side of the bed. Luckily, it was the short man – and in his way was the hospital trolley. Dom dodged to the side, unsteady on his feet and still woozy from the anaesthetic. The man leaned across the trolley, trying to grab Dom. His fingers snatched at Dom's hospital gown.

Dom kicked out at the side of the trolley. The force of his kick sent it crashing backwards, knocking the man flying.

The woman was on her feet again. She grabbed a syringe that lay in a metal tray on the table at the end of the bed. Dom grabbed the nearest thing to hand. It was the jug of water. He swung it in a rising arc – up into her chin. Water sloshed out, and the woman's head snapped back under the impact of the blow. But she had the syringe. She jabbed it towards Dom. He stepped back, his feet cold and wet from the spilled water.

He hurled the jug at the woman. The rest of the water cascaded out as the jug bounced off the woman's arm. She ignored it and rushed at him, holding the syringe in front of her like a lance.

Dom was pressed against the bedside cabinet. There was no way he could dodge out of the way of the syringe. The short man was still on the floor, but watching and laughing as the woman came at Dom. Her own face was twisted into a cruel smile.

Then she gave a cry of surprise. Her feet had slipped on the water from the jug. She staggered and tried to regain her balance, but fell.

Dom didn't hesitate. He leaped over the fallen woman, skidding in the puddle of water as he landed. But he was expecting that, and his bare feet gripped the smooth floor better than the woman's shoes. Within a moment, he was across the room and out into the corridor. He slammed the door behind him. There was a bolt at the top of the door and another at the bottom. He pushed home the bottom bolt, but couldn't reach the one at the top. He didn't waste time trying. He ran.

They had not seen the whole place when they did the tour, and Dom hadn't really been paying attention anyway. And now he had no idea where he was going. He just wanted to get out. Behind him, the doctor and nurse – if they really were a doctor and nurse – were hammering on the door and shouting for help. Dom kept running.

He rushed along the corridor, round a corner. There were footsteps hurrying the other way, coming towards him, drawn by the sound of his running. Dom ducked into the nearest doorway. The door was slightly open, and he tumbled through. He leaped back to his feet and pushed the door almost closed. Through the small crack between the door and its frame, Dom watched as the fair-haired man ran past.

Dom was out of breath already. He didn't know how long he had been kept here. He had no idea how long it was since he last had any exercise – even walking. Now he'd stopped, his legs felt weak and flimsy. He needed to find somewhere to hide until they gave up the search for him. Then maybe he could sneak out.

He turned away from the door, looking to see if there was anywhere to hide in the room. He had to be quick, because he could already hear the sound of people coming.

It looked like a hospital ward. There were two rows of beds just like the one Dom had been in. Three beds in each row, so six in all. Each bed had a sheet pulled up over it, covering what must be piles of blankets and pillows. With luck, the room was unused. With luck, they wouldn't look for him in here.

But the fair-haired man was coming back. He was shouting, presumably at the man and woman that Dom had escaped from. Angry voices getting closer and closer.

'He's a child – what is he, thirteen? How can you let a thirteen-year-old get the better of you?'

The other, shorter, man muttered a reply that Dom couldn't hear.

'He took us by surprise,' the woman protested. 'He's a cunning one.'

'We'll have to be methodical. Check every room. I want him found.'

This time, Dom did hear what the other man said: 'Don't worry about it. We'll find him. It's not like he's going anywhere, is it?'

A door was pushed open nearby. They would check this room soon. Dom looked around desperately. There was nowhere to hide – if he crawled under a bed, they'd see him as soon as they walked in, and the cupboards were far too small.

A shadow passed across the crack between the door and its frame. Dom didn't think; he just dived for the only possible hiding place.

The door creaked open.

'Not in here,' the woman's voice said. It was filtered by the flimsy material of the sheet.

'He'll be in there soon enough,' the fair-haired man said.

'Quiet as the grave,' the other man said, and they all laughed. There was a click as the door closed.

Dom wasn't laughing. He wasn't even relieved that they hadn't found him. He was lying terrified under the sheet on one of the beds. He had expected to have to press close to a pile of blankets and a pillow. But that wasn't what was concealed beneath the sheet.

He was lying beside a body.

As soon as he heard the door close, Dom rolled off the bed. The sheet was pulled sideways, exposing the face of the body on the bed. Eyes stared glassily from the deathly pale face.

'Dave?' Dom whispered.

There was no response. Dom's hand was shaking as he reached out and touched the boy's cheek. It was cold as ice. Swallowing back his fear, Dom pulled the sheet back over the body. He had to get out of here. He didn't look under the other sheets because he knew what he would find. There had been seven children on the visit. Dom had never been much good at maths, but he knew he was the only one left.

He couldn't hear the fair-haired man shouting any more. Dom hoped that meant they had moved on down the corridor. He slipped out of the room and headed back the way he had come – the opposite way to where they were now searching for him.

The door to the room they had kept him in stood open. It would be the last place they would search for him, but Dom didn't want to go back in there. Just the thought of returning to that room made him feel sick.

He carried on down the corridor. There were no more rooms this way, and the corridor soon ended in a door. That was how they'd known he didn't go that way, Dom realised. The door was bolted from this side with a wide strip of metal slotted into a bracket on the wall to make sure no one could open it from the other side. They knew he couldn't have gone through and bolted it behind him.

On the other side of the door was a wide concrete stairway leading downwards. Pale light filtered up from below. There was no way Dom could bolt the door behind him. He just hoped they wouldn't check this way again. Perhaps the door was bolted because the stairs led to a way out … He pulled the door closed as quietly as he could, but even so it banged back against its frame, the sound echoing ominously down the concrete stairwell.

Hope rising with every step, Dom tiptoed down the stairs. The air seemed to change as he descended. It was getting close and musty. There was a strange earthy smell to it.

The steps ended in a huge, open area. It was like an underground aircraft hangar. The ceiling was much higher than Dom expected and he realised the area must extend up into the rest of the building above, and the floor was below ground level. He couldn't see the end of the chamber. There were several wall lights close to the bottom of the stairs, but the area was soon lost in darkness and shadow.

If he felt his way along the wall, Dom decided, he might find another door – a way out.

But what he actually found was a metal bar. Then another. As his eyes gradually adjusted to the gloom, he could see that there was a line of the bars stretching into the distance. The bars cut off a large section of the space, like a huge prison cell.

He stood staring into the darkness, desperately hoping to see the dark rectangle of a doorway. His hand brushed along the wall beside the bars, knocking against a large switch. Did he dare turn the lights on? He hesitated, hand on the switch.

At that moment, he heard the door at the top of the stairs bang shut again. Then he heard the sound of footsteps descending rapidly.

'He must be down here,' the fair-haired man called. 'Come on!' There was anger and urgency and something else in his voice. Was it fear?

Dom had to get out – now. He didn't think about it, just pressed down on the large switch. He was ready to screw up his eyes against the sudden glare of the lights.

But the lights didn't come on.

There was a metallic scraping sound – even louder than the approaching footsteps. Even louder than the worried shouts. He heard the woman cry out, and this time the fear was unmistakable.

Movement. It took Dom a few seconds to work out what it was. In the dim light, it seemed like the dark space between the first bar and the wall was widening. But then he realised that the bars were sliding away from him, like a huge door opening. Dom walked slowly, following the moving bars, wondering what was behind them – a way out? *Escape?*

There was another noise now. A snuffling, rasping buzz that reminded Dom of a cat purring. Only much, much louder. The musty, hot smell in the air grew stronger, and deeper.

The fair-haired man was shouting, running across from the stairs. The short man and the woman were close behind him. Then the woman stopped and put her hand out to halt the short man too. They were both staring transfixed at Dom.

He realised the fair-haired man wasn't running towards him. He was running towards where the bars had been – heading for the switch. He was yelling and shouting, but Dom couldn't hear what he was saying.

He couldn't hear because the purring sound was so loud. There was a feeling of warm air on the back of Dom's neck. A breeze from outside? He'd done it – he'd found a way out. Ignoring the running man, Dom turned quickly to face the darkness.

Except that the darkness was now filled with another shape – huge and glistening. Enormous watery eyes caught the sparse light as they stared down at Dom. The purring became a roar. The warm air was rancid and foul and smelled of rotting meat. The eyes grew bigger, closer.

The fair-haired man skidded to a halt, still metres away from the switch. The terror on his face was the most frightening thing Dom had ever seen. The reason it was so frightening was that he knew it was mirrored on his own face.

The man turned to run, but Dom could see that he already knew it was pointless. There was nowhere to go.

Chapter 1

'Things can't get much worse,' Owen said to himself. That was his first big mistake of the day. Though, in fact, things seemed about to get a whole lot better. After a week, he was finally escaping. He was even looking forward to going back to school.

The sun was beating down on the deck of the boat. Vicky was in the cabin with her Uncle Andy, so Owen didn't have to talk to either of them – though he didn't think Vicky was talking to him today anyway. They were cousins, but a week ago they had hardly known each other. A week ago, Owen had thought the chance to spend February half-term with Vicky on her uncle's own private island was the coolest thing he could imagine. Not only that, but he'd be able to get away from his annoying little brother for a week.

It never occurred to him that it would be cold and wet and boring on an island off the north coast of Scotland. He didn't know that Uncle Andy would spend most of the time on email and the phone running his company, which was based on the nearby mainland. Or that Uncle Andy would be such a pain.

He'd never seen before what a pain Vicky was either.

The couple of times they'd met at family events, he'd thought she was clever. But whether she was clever or not, she was more interested in her uncle than in Owen. And her uncle seemed interested in no one but himself. So for the past week it had been all 'Oh, Uncle Andy, you're so wonderful' and 'I think that's just marvellous'. He wasn't even her real uncle – he was Vicky's stepmother's brother.

But whatever the connection, as far as both Uncle Andy and Vicky were concerned, Owen might as well have been invisible. Vicky seemed to ignore him the whole week. He wondered why she wanted him there at all. So Owen had to spend a long week with Vicky and lovely, adorable, marvellous Uncle Andy, stuck on an island with no books and being pretty much ignored.

By the time they left on Uncle Andy's expensive boat (the exact price of it mentioned at every opportunity) to sail back to the mainland, Owen was ready to jump up and down and punch the air in celebration. The sun came out as the boat pulled away from the quay, and he took that as a sign that things were definitely getting better.

A few hours later, he wondered if he could possibly have been more wrong.

The storm blew up out of nowhere. One minute there were blue skies and a refreshing breeze that blew the yacht briskly through the calm waters; the next, dark clouds were amassing and the wind was becoming a gale. The first heavy drops of rain blew into Owen's face. The boat was lurching and rocking.

Uncle Andy appeared from the cabin. 'You'd better come inside. Could be a bit choppy. It's fine for me and Vicky, but you're not used to it. We don't want you being seasick on the woodwork.' His words were almost lost in the noise of the wind and the crash of the water against the boat.

'No, we don't want that,' Owen muttered. He was pretty sure it was the woodwork that Uncle Andy was worried about rather than his health. All week Uncle Andy had told him what to do and how to do it – or what not to do and how not to do it. He seemed to assume that Owen was completely useless at everything and had never done anything. 'If you turn your fork over, you'll find it easier to eat the peas.' Or: 'Don't forget to clean your teeth.' And Owen's favourite: 'I'll have to ask Vicky if you like cabbage.' As if Owen didn't know himself what he liked and what he didn't.

Owen felt awkward and bulky in his life jacket, but now he was glad to be wearing it. Although it was a large boat, there was barely room for all three of them in the cabin. Owen was pressed uncomfortably close to Vicky. She glared at him like the weather was his fault.

'You up to holding the wheel?' Uncle Andy asked.

It took Owen a moment to realise the question was addressed to him. 'Yes – I guess so.'

'I think even you should manage it. Just hold it steady – can you do that? Don't let her turn.'

'I'll cope,' Owen told him. How difficult could it be?

But Uncle Andy obviously wasn't expecting a reply and was speaking again. 'Vicky and I will haul the sails down before the wind gets too strong. We could lose control otherwise.'

Vicky looked anxious. 'But we'll be all right?'

Uncle Andy nodded. 'Of course we will. Just need to lower the sails and then we'll sit this out. It won't last long. Worst case, we use the motors.'

The wind was even stronger now, and Vicky had to fight the door to get it open as the wind tried to blow it shut again. Uncle Andy leaned past her to help push, and the two of them struggled outside.

Owen was glad to be inside the cabin, though it didn't offer much protection. The wheel was twisting in his grip, as if trying to break free of him. It took all of Owen's strength to hold it almost still.

Rain was washing down the windows so he could barely see. The sound of the wind was getting louder. Out of the side windows, Owen could make out the shapes of Vicky and her uncle as they struggled with ropes and heaved at the main sail. Slowly but surely it was coming down. The boat seemed to settle slightly. The wheel was less difficult to hold.

He blew out a long breath of relief. Things weren't so bad after all. Then Owen glanced out of the window on the other side of the cabin – and saw a wall of water rushing towards him.

He had no time to react. The wave crashed into the boat, knocking Owen off his feet. Glass from the broken window flew past his face as the water poured in. He struggled to get up, slipped and tried again.

The cabin door was hanging in its frame, splintered and broken. Owen forced his way past the jagged wood and out on to the deck. It was awash, with water round his ankles as the boat pitched and turned. He slipped again, grabbing a rope for support and feeling it bite into his hands as he tried to hold on.

'Vicky!' he yelled. But even Owen couldn't hear his own voice above the crash of the water and the howl of the wind.

He blinked rain and salt water out of his eyes. He thought he could see her, holding on to the bottom of the mast. Was that Uncle Andy beside her? Their life jackets were blurred smudges of orange. As he watched, Owen saw one of the orange smudges slide away from the other and slam into the rail at the side of the boat.

Owen was panicking now. He had no idea what to do. If he tried to help, he'd probably be swept over the side. But if not, then Vicky and her uncle could suffer the same fate. He looked around, desperately hoping to see a coil of rope so he could lash himself to the rail that went around the cabin. But there was nothing – just seawater and rain and wind stinging his face.

Above the terrible sound of the storm there was a sudden crack like thunder. Except it wasn't thunder. Owen watched in helpless disbelief as the boat's mast bent and broke. The huge wooden pole toppled slowly towards him. He dived out of the way as the mast slammed into the cabin, crushing the roof. The surviving windows shattered.

Owen was sliding on his side across the deck. He could see the crumpled shape of Uncle Andy against the side rail. Vicky's terrified face stared at him as she clung to the broken bottom of the mast. The ripped sail was strewn across the deck and over Vicky. If she got entangled in it, she'd stand no chance against the violence of the sea.

Managing to brace himself against the side rail, Owen struggled to his feet. He stumbled across the lurching deck towards Vicky. She reached out towards him. Her fair hair was dark with the wet and plastered back from her pale face. Her eyes were wide and frightened. Somehow he managed to force his way against the wind and grabbed her hand. She let go of the mast and fell on to him, her weight sending them both sliding across the deck.

'It's all right – I've got you,' he told her. She didn't react. Maybe she didn't hear.

With a shattering crash, the front of the boat suddenly rose upwards, sending the two of them sliding towards the back of the boat. Then it smashed down again. Down further than Owen thought possible. The deck beside him exploded, splinters and fragments of wood whipping past his face.

'We've hit the rocks,' Vicky yelled.

Chapter 2

Ragged, grey stone was jutting up from the punctured deck. Vicky was right – the boat had crashed on to rocks. Water was bubbling up round the rocks as the boat shifted and began to sink.

'We have to get out,' Vicky shouted.

'But where do we go?' Owen could swim, but he didn't think he could make it through a storm to the mainland – it must be miles away.

A sudden shaft of sunlight cut through the dark clouds. It lit up a forest of rocks sticking up out of the water. And beyond them – land. A beach. They were too far from the mainland; they must have crashed on another island.

The sunlight spread slowly across the water, which seemed to be calming. The rain was easing, the spray dropping.

Vicky pulled free of Owen's grasp and unsteadily got to her feet. 'If you'd kept hold of the wheel like Uncle Andy said …'

'Then I'd be in there,' Owen told her, pointing to the wrecked cabin, the mast lying across its shattered remains.

'I suppose,' she admitted, looking around. 'Where is –'
She broke off as she saw him. 'Uncle Andy!'

He was still lying against the side rail. Vicky ran to him, slipping and skidding on the wet deck.

At least, Owen thought, the boat didn't actually seem to be sinking. But the hull was broken and it was stuck fast. It was groaning and creaking as the waves pushed it against the rocks. Owen's whole body ached and hurt like he'd been hit with hundreds of hammers. He was cold and wet, shivering maybe from shock as well. He stumbled after Vicky.

Although Uncle Andy's eyes were closed, his chest was moving as he breathed. There was blood across his forehead, but otherwise he didn't seem injured.

'We have to get help,' Vicky said.

'We have to get off this boat,' Owen told her. 'If the storm comes back, the sea will break it to pieces against these rocks. We'll have to carry him.'

Between them, they somehow managed to lift Uncle Andy and get him to the other side of the boat, closer to the shore. The rail on this side had broken away, and they could just about walk out across the rocks, which were wet and slippery. But with care, and as the wind dropped, the two of them were able to get Uncle Andy to the shore. He stirred and mumbled but didn't wake.

'We can't just leave him,' Vicky said.

'We can't carry him much further,' Owen pointed out. They were exhausted just from getting him ashore. 'Besides – we have to get up there.'

The beach ended at steep cliffs. Owen reckoned they could climb up, but they couldn't do it carrying Uncle Andy.

'What if the tide comes in?' Vicky asked.

'It doesn't come right up to the cliffs,' Owen told her. 'There's grass and wild flowers at the foot of the cliffs, look. We'll drag him up there and then I'll go for help.'

'Help from where?'

'I don't know,' he told her, exasperated. 'But we can't just sit here and hope someone comes along.'

'We must be on one of the other islands. What if there's no one here?'

Owen sighed. She was being so negative, but she had a point. 'There must be someone,' he told her. He pointed up at the top of the cliffs. 'It looks like there's a fence at the top, so someone must have put it there.'

Vicky didn't look convinced. 'Could have been years ago.'

'I'll be as quick as I can,' Owen assured her. 'Let's get him to the bottom of the cliffs. Just stay put there till I'm back.'

'Are you mad? I'm not staying here. I'm coming with you.'

'But your uncle …'

'We'll leave him a note.'

'Oh, brought your pad and paper, have you?'

'We can call for help. I've got my mobile …' She pulled it out from inside her life jacket with a flourish. But then her face fell. 'Dead. Must have got too wet.'

Owen was ashamed he hadn't even thought of that. But his own mobile was just as dead. The screen was cracked and water spilled out of it.

They checked Uncle Andy's pockets, but couldn't find his phone. There was a radio on the boat, but it was in the crushed cabin.

'You should stay with him,' Owen decided. It made sense and, anyway, he'd rather be on his own.

'No way.'

'But if he wakes up and wonders where we are –'

Vicky interrupted him. 'We'll leave our life jackets. He'll work out that means we got ashore and we're OK and have gone for help.'

'And what if he doesn't?'

'He will,' she insisted. 'We can write a note in the sand: "Gone for help – V and O". Now come on, we're wasting time.'

The sand under the cliffs was sheltered from the rain, but the note would wash away in no time if the rain got heavier or the wind changed direction. But Owen didn't bother to tell Vicky that. He could see there was no point in arguing, and she was right – the sooner they got started, the better. He was cold and wet and just wanted to get home. He guessed Vicky probably felt the same.

It wasn't as difficult to get up the cliffs as Owen had feared. But, even so, there was no way they'd have been able to drag Uncle Andy up with them. It was hard work – the cliffs were steep, and, though it was wet, the soft sand slipped under their feet. Owen silently cursed Vicky as he grabbed her arm to stop her from falling. But a few minutes later, it was her arm round his waist as he slipped that saved him from a nasty tumble.

'Thanks,' Owen muttered.

Vicky smiled thinly. Her wet hair was blown across her face, which Owen knew would annoy her. She spent forever washing and brushing her hair to get it just right. For the first time, he felt sorry for her – the first emotion apart from irritation and anger he'd felt for her all week.

'Come on,' she said, pushing on up the cliff. 'Almost there now.'

Neither of them commented that the wooden fence at the top of the cliff was broken and rotted. Vicky's fears were confirmed – it had been there for years.

'Which way?' she asked.

There was no path. Owen shrugged and said, 'I guess we just walk in a straight line. Head inland, I'd say. We must get somewhere eventually: a road or a track or a path or something.'

The rain had become a steady drizzle. It hung in the air, damp and clammy against the skin. Owen could feel it seeping through his clothes. Slowly, it seemed to solidify, blotting out the sun. The air thickened into mist, and the whole world was a uniform grey.

'We'll never see anything in this,' Vicky pointed out.

'You're right,' Owen admitted reluctantly. 'We could walk right past a farmhouse and not notice.'

'Maybe we should go back to Uncle Andy.' Her voice trembled slightly. Owen hadn't realised how frightened she was.

He hadn't realised how frightened he was either. But Vicky's words reminded him that he didn't really know which way they had come. In the heavy mist, they could be walking in circles. Getting back to Uncle Andy was as difficult as keeping going and looking for help.

But before he could reply, an unearthly sound split the air. It was like the roar of some huge animal, though Owen couldn't begin to think what.

Vicky grabbed his arm. 'What was that?'

Owen shook his head. He had no answer. The sound had faded, but in the distance he thought he could hear a growling.

'A lorry?' Vicky asked. Her eyes were wide. 'Farm machinery?'

'Could be,' he told her. But he didn't believe it.

'Which way did it come from?'

'I don't know. This mist sort of deadens the sound. It seemed to come from all round us. Maybe it was the sea against the rocks, if the storm's getting up again.'

It didn't sound convincing. They'd taken several paces before Owen realised that Vicky was holding his hand. He said nothing, and they kept walking. Before long Owen noticed that the ground under his feet had become firmer and more level. They were on a narrow tarmacked road or track.

Then suddenly she pulled her hand away. She clasped it over her mouth and gasped in fear and surprise.

A dark shape loomed out of the mist. It was coming straight for them. Owen turned quickly. But another dark shape emerged from the damp, grey air beside them. And another. Slowly, the shapeless figures closed in.

Owen and Vicky were surrounded.

Chapter 3

The figures seemed to solidify out of the mist.

'They're just … children,' Vicky said.

The nearest figure laughed, but there was a cruel edge to the sound. 'Who are you calling children?' the boy demanded. He looked about fourteen now that Owen could see him clearly. 'How old are you – ten?'

'Shut up, Ed,' a girl said from behind Owen. Like the boy, she was wearing jeans and walking boots. Her dark hair was cut short, clinging damply to her head with a few stray strands across her cheeks. She had a thick waterproof jacket zipped up to her neck and she wore a small rucksack on her back.

'Are you camping?' Owen asked.

Another boy answered, stepping through the mist. 'No, we're running a pizza-delivery service.'

'Really?' Vicky said.

Her incredulous tone made the teenagers laugh. There were three boys and two girls, all about fourteen or fifteen years old – older than Owen and Vicky.

'That's enough of that,' a deep voice said. 'What's going on?'

A tall, well-built man stepped appeared behind the teenagers.

'Found some kids, Mr Gardner,' the first boy said, the one the girl had called Ed. He made 'kids' sound like an insult.

The man regarded Owen and Vicky curiously. He had close-cut, dark hair and the beginnings of a beard. His eyes were deep set, making him look slightly sinister in the misty light.

'Bit young to be out hiking on your own, aren't you? And not really dressed for it either.'

'We're not hiking,' Vicky told him. 'We were in a boat.'

'A boat?'

'They're pirates – ooh arrrr!' Ed said, covering one of his eyes with his hand, like an eye patch. 'Show us your wooden leg, girlie.'

'Oh, do be quiet,' Vicky told him.

'*Oh, do be quiet,*' one of the other girls echoed, mimicking Vicky's tone. She was dark-skinned, her black hair in tight plaits. 'Posh, ain't ya? Got a boat and everything.'

'Not any more,' Owen told her. 'It smashed on the rocks.'

'You're not hurt?' the man asked at once. He sounded concerned.

Owen saw tears welling up in Vicky's eyes as she replied. 'My uncle – we left him on the beach. He's …' She choked on the words, unable to go on.

'Cry baby,' Ed muttered. He was fair-haired, his mouth a cruel slash across his face that was more like a cut.

The man – Mr Gardner – glared at Ed and put his hand on Vicky's shoulder. 'It's all right now. You're safe here, and we'll see what we can do for your uncle. Is he hurt?'

'Just knocked out, I think,' Owen said. He was surprised to hear that his own voice was trembling.

Mr Gardner nodded. 'You know the way back to where you left him?'

Owen nodded. But then he looked at how thick the mist had become, and he wondered if he really did. 'Maybe.'

'Lucky to find anything in this. Hopefully it'll lift soon, then we can search.'

'We can't just leave him,' Vicky said.

'Do you know how to get back to him?' the short-haired girl who'd first spoken asked.

Vicky shook her head.

'We'll keep following the track,' Mr Gardner decided. 'That'll take us to the research station. We can get in touch with the mainland from there and organise a helicopter as soon as this mist lifts. They'll have a first-aid kit there too. Don't worry, it's not far.'

'You've been saying that for hours,' Ed complained.

'It must be true then,' one of the other two boys said. He grinned, and Owen saw that one of his front teeth was broken. His hair was a tousled mess and his jeans were torn.

'Shut up, Mikey,' Ed muttered.

Mr Gardner led the way, and Owen and Vicky walked with him. The other children followed behind, muttering and arguing among themselves. There was rain mixed in with the mist – cold, sharp rain. It was turning to sleet, and Owen wondered if it was going to snow. The warm, sunny day when he'd set out on Uncle Andy's boat seemed years ago.

'They don't mean any harm,' Mr Gardner said quietly as they made their way along the track.

'Are you on a school trip or something?' Owen asked.

The girl with the plaits was close enough to hear and laughed at that.

'Not exactly, though I am a teacher. Thank you, Jude,' he added as the girl laughed again.

'I ain't been to school for years,' she replied. She sounded proud of the fact.

'Then what?' Vicky asked.

'I steal stuff,' Jude told her. 'Can't help it, I just do. Mikey …' She pointed to the boy with curly dark hair and torn jeans. 'He's the same, except he burns things down.'

'Yes, thank you, Jude, that'll do,' Mr Gardner snapped. 'This is a team-building thing,' he explained. 'Or it's supposed to be. To teach them how to work together, to learn the value of other people. They're all kids who've …' He paused, as if thinking of how to say it. 'Who have had problems,' he said at last.

Vicky's eyes were wide. 'What sort of problems?' she asked in a hushed whisper.

'It varies,' Mr Gardner said awkwardly, obviously unwilling to discuss it.

But Jude was happy to tell them. 'I told you about me and Mikey. Ed is just a bit …' She glanced at him. 'Well, he loses his temper easily.'

From the way she said it, Owen guessed Ed was a violent bully as well as a rude loudmouth.

The mist was gone and the sleet was getting heavier. From somewhere ahead of them in the rain came the ominous rumbling roar of sound that Owen and Vicky had heard earlier. It seemed closer now.

Owen saw Mr Gardner frown. 'What is that?' he asked.

The man shook his head. 'Wish I knew. Sounds almost … alive.' He gave a short laugh. 'I wish the weather would cheer up.' He pulled a hood up from his waterproof. 'You OK?'

Owen and Vicky were both cold and soaked. But Owen didn't think he could ask to borrow anyone's waterproof. 'We're fine.'

'So long as this place we're going isn't far,' Vicky said.

'Should be nearly there, I think.'

Mr Gardner turned and glanced at the bedraggled figures following. Owen turned too. It was a little easier to see through the sleet than it had been through the mist. But not much.

'So who's the other girl?' Owen asked Jude as they started walking again.

'Tam – Tamara. Her problem's computers.'

'Steals them?' Vicky asked.

'Steals things *with* them. Movies, music, other people's data. Then last – and definitely least – is Brendan.'

Owen frowned. He'd counted the figures through the rain just now when he turned. Three of them were following – Tam, and then Ed and Mikey were the only boys. He looked back again. 'I don't see Brendan,' he told Jude.

She sighed and called out, 'Mr Gardner – Brendan's not there.'

'What?'

Mr Gardner stopped. The others slowly caught up. Mikey leaned over, his hands on his knees as he caught his breath.

'Where's Brendan?' asked Mr Gardner.

They all looked around, but there was no sign of anyone else.

'Brendan!' Ed yelled. 'Stop messing about – we're over here!'

'Where are you?' Mikey shouted. 'Loser!'

'I'll go back and find him,' Jude said.

'No, Jude, I don't think –' Mr Gardner started.

But she was already walking quickly back down the narrow track. 'I won't leave the path. Just give me a minute, all right?'

Before long she had disappeared into the sleet.

'He wouldn't have wandered off,' Mr Gardner said. He sounded anxious.

'I would, given the chance,' Ed muttered.

'Bren wouldn't though,' Tam told him. 'He was scared. Didn't like the fog.'

'Didn't like anything,' Mikey added, straightening up. 'Come on, Jude!' he shouted down the track.

'We'd better go back and find them both,' Mr Gardner decided. 'Come on.'

They trudged back through the mist for several minutes, calling out to Brendan and Jude. But there was no answer.

'What's that?' Tam said suddenly. She ran ahead, disappearing into the gloom.

'Not you too – come back!' Mr Gardner shouted.

Tam came back a moment later carrying something. It looked like an old sack, torn and ripped. As she rejoined them, Owen saw that it was the remains of a rucksack, caked in mud and stained. One of the straps was broken, the other ended in a ragged tear. It looked familiar.

'It's Jude's,' Tam said, breathless.

As soon as she said it, Owen remembered the girl had been wearing it. Or a rucksack very similar.

'But there's no sign of her, or of Brendan,' Tam went on. 'This was just lying there at the side of the track. I think …' She swallowed and held it so the torn-off end of strap hung down. She touched the strap nervously with her finger, then showed them all the dark stain on the end of her finger.

'I think it's blood,' she said.

Chapter 4

Mr Gardner told the rest of them to stay where they were while he went back down the track with Tam to look for the missing Brendan and Jude.

'I'm sure they're fine,' Mr Gardner said, but the look on his face didn't match his reassuring words. 'We won't be long. Just stay here. All of you,' he added, glaring at Ed.

Ed glared back but said nothing. As soon as Mr Gardner and Tam were out of sight, Ed shrugged off his rucksack and sat down on the wet grass as the side of the track. Mikey joined him.

Realising how tired he was, Owen sat down too.

Vicky leaned against him at the side of the track. 'What are we going to do?' she demanded.

'Stay here, like he said. Then get to this research station and they can help us find your uncle and get him some medical treatment.'

'What do they research?' Vicky wondered, pulling at a tuft of wet grass.

'Something boring,' Ed replied. 'Waste of time. We should have stayed at the campsite.'

'In the storm?' Mikey said. 'We need shelter. The weather's not getting any better.'

'It's snowing now,' Vicky pointed out.

She was right. The sleet was solidifying into snow. It wasn't fluffy, Christmas-card snow. It was wet and freezing cold and stinging Owen's face. He had to blink it out of his eyes as it got thicker.

'Won't even be able to see the track soon,' Mikey said.

'Oh great,' Vicky complained. 'We might be lost here forever.'

'You wouldn't be the first,' a voice announced loudly.

It had a heavy Scottish accent, and it came from just behind Owen. He jumped to his feet in surprise.

A tall but stooped figure was standing behind them, just visible through the snow. He stepped forward, and it was impossible to tell if his hair was brilliant white or if the snow had settled on it and hidden its true colour.

'Who are you?' Ed demanded.

'As if it's any of your business,' the man told him.

'Do you live here, sir?' Vicky asked.

'*Sir?*' Ed snorted.

The man ignored him. 'Hereabouts. Nice to see one of you's got some manners. You got a grown-up with you?'

'Mr Gardner,' Owen told him. 'He'll be back in a minute.'

'Gardner should know his way about. Taking you up to the research station, is he?'

'That's right,' Vicky said.

The man nodded, snow slipping from his forehead. 'Best place to be. Closer than my farm. It's not as homely up there, but you'll be warm and dry at the research station. If you make it.'

'What do you mean, if we make it?' Vicky asked.

Even Mikey lifted his head to hear the answer.

'Oh, don't you worry about it,' the man said. Owen thought he was smiling, but couldn't be sure through the thickening snow. 'It's just old stories, that's all. Myths and legends, tales and rumours.'

'What is?' Vicky asked nervously.

'People going missing in the mist or disappearing without trace in the snow. Just stupid local talk.'

'Brendan,' Mikey said quietly. 'And Jude.'

'Hasn't happened in a while, though,' the man went on, not having heard. 'But you hear and see strange things when you're out on the moorland. Don't you stray from this path, now, will you?'

'Not likely,' Vicky told him.

'Good girl. Need to keep you safe and well for –' He broke off and sucked a loud breath of cold air through his teeth. 'For all our sakes,' he finished.

'What do you mean?' Ed asked.

'Kids like you – they're the future, aren't they? That's what the media keeps telling us. Got to get you properly educated and all that. Investing in our own futures, so they tell us.' He looked at Mikey, who grinned back, showing off his broken tooth. 'God help us,' the man added.

'You said you hear strange things,' Owen said. 'Do you mean, like, stories?'

'Them too. But out on the moors, you hear things that can't always be explained. Oh, they say it's the roar of the sea or the wail of the wind. And maybe it is. Or perhaps it's the wail of young Jimmie Foster who went missing when he was about your age and was never seen again. Him, or what's left of him – his spirit.'

'A ghost?' Vicky said. She clutched at Owen's shoulder.

'And the roar of the sea,' Owen said. 'We heard … well, it sounded like a roar, like an animal, but it must have been the sea, mustn't it?'

'You're a long way from the coast now,' the man told him. 'The path's been heading away from it for a good mile or more.'

'But the noise,' Mikey said. 'We all heard it. It has to be the sea, doesn't it?'

The man was definitely smiling now. 'Of course. Don't you pay no heed to the stories. The roar of the sea. The sound of the waves crashing down on the shore. What else could it be?'

'As soon as Mr Gardner is back, we make for the research station,' Mikey said. 'As fast as we can.'

Ed's face twisted into a sneer. But it didn't last, and Owen could tell he was nervous too.

'Good idea, lad,' the old man agreed. 'Best not to be out in the open when it's like this. It'll only get worse.'

'The sooner we're off this island, the better,' Ed said.

The man laughed at that. 'You won't be getting off the island any time soon, lad. This weather's set in now. No one can get here and no one can leave, not for a few days.'

'Days?' Vicky echoed in disbelief.

'At least. It lasts weeks, sometimes.'

The sound of approaching voices made them all turn. Tam and Mr Gardner appeared through the snow. It was settling now, dusting the path with a thin carpet of white.

'Where're Bren and Jude?' Mikey asked. 'Did you find them?'

Tam shook her head.

'No sign of them,' Mr Gardner said. 'Just have to hope they have the sense to follow the path and join us at the research station.'

'Maybe the man saw them?' Vicky suggested.

'What man?' Mr Gardner asked.

But the old man was gone. He had disappeared as suddenly and silently as he had arrived – fading into the snowy air like a ghost.

Chapter 5

The snow got steadily heavier and thicker. It didn't seem as cold, but maybe Owen was just getting used to it. Thick, woolly flakes hung in the air as they trudged onwards. Soon the ground was covered, and it became harder to see the track. Several times, one or other of the group stumbled at the edge where the tarmac gave way to snow-covered grass.

Mr Gardner had given Vicky his coat because she was so cold. Owen was cold too, but he couldn't imagine Ed or any of the other teenagers giving up their coat for him. And he wasn't going to ask.

They were climbing uphill, the track winding in a large circle. Above them, through the snow, Owen thought he could make out the shape of a building. It was dark and hard-edged in the soft white world of the blizzard.

'That must be it,' Mr Gardner said. He sounded wary and nervous rather than relieved.

'I thought you'd been here before,' Ed said.

'I have. Of course I have.' Mr Gardner had to shout over the howl of the wind. 'But it's hard to see in the snow.'

They stumbled onwards, up the hill, with their heads down as they struggled into the wind. Owen only looked up when he heard Vicky gasp. It took a moment to work out what he was looking at. The dark shape in front of them seemed to make no sense, until Mikey said, 'It must have skidded in the snow.'

A large four-by-four was at an angle, half on and half off the track. Its bonnet was buried in a high metal fence. The fence itself was twisted and torn, not just where the vehicle had hit it but for a good few metres either side.

'It's not been snowing that long,' Ed told him. 'If this just happened, we'd have heard.'

'Maybe we did,' Tam suggested. 'That roaring sound.'

'What about the fence?' Mikey said. 'That wasn't done by the crash.'

Mr Gardner had run up to the crumpled vehicle. As they got closer, Owen saw that the whole of one side had been ripped away. The windscreen was shattered, and he could make out a figure slumped inside. He took Vicky's hand, holding her back. He dreaded what Mr Gardner might find.

When Mr Gardner returned after a few moments, his face was grave. Even against the constantly falling snow, he looked pale.

'Let's get inside,' he said.

'The driver?' Ed asked.

'Nothing to be done for him now.'

'But why would they just leave him there?' Vicky asked, her voice shaking.

'There's something very wrong,' Mr Gardner agreed. 'Let's get out of the snow and find someone.'

Mikey was facing the other way, looking back along the fence. 'That's not good,' he said, pointing.

The track continued on the other side of the fence. There was a wide metal gate that Owen assumed was normally closed over the track. Maybe it was automatic or operated from inside the research station. It was as tall as the fence and would have been just as impregnable.

Except that it was sagging, twisted and broken. It looked as though some giant hand had reached down and torn it away from its fixings, crumpling and dropping it.

'What could do that?' Vicky asked quietly.

Owen didn't answer. He kept hold of Vicky's hand as they followed Mr Gardner up the track to the building.

The research station was a plain, grey, concrete block with narrow windows. Like the gate, the main doors of the building had been wrenched open and torn from their hinges. Mr Gardner said nothing as he led them through, but the others all exchanged worried looks.

'What the hell happened here?' Ed wondered out loud.

'Nothing good,' Tam told him.

The doors opened into a large reception area. The whole place was lit by the dull red glow of emergency lighting, and it was a mess. The reception desk had been overturned, which had sent papers and a computer flying. A coffee mug lay in fragments by a wall that had a long crack down it. Papers blew across the floor, and snow was drifting in.

Mr Gardner grabbed two coats from pegs on the wall and threw one across to Owen.

'Thanks.' He struggled into it. The coat was too big and he had to rolls the cuffs back so the sleeves didn't dangle over his hands. Mr Gardner put the other coat on. He knelt down beside a telephone that had fallen from the desk.

Ed had crossed to the doors leading from the reception area deeper into the building. 'You should see this,' he said to Mr Gardner. His voice sounded strained.

'What?' Mr Gardner looked up from the telephone. 'Dead,' he muttered, dropping it back to the floor.

'So are these guys,' Ed told him.

Two men in white coats lay sprawled on the floor of the corridor. The children picked their way carefully past the bodies. Mr Gardner quickly checked each, but even Owen could see there was nothing to be done. The men's white lab coats were torn and stained with blood, which almost seemed to glow in the red light. Their eyes were staring sightless and terrified.

Owen could feel his breath catch in his throat. Vicky gasped and turned away. The fear and horror Tam and Mikey felt was obvious in their expressions.

'It looks like something tried to *eat* them,' Ed said. He sounded as appalled and frightened as the rest of them.

Even Mr Gardner looked pale. 'Right,' he announced, 'we need to find a phone that works, and we need to see if there's anyone else here.'

'Should we split up?' Mikey asked.

'It'll be quicker,' Mr Gardner agreed.

'Won't be safer,' Ed pointed out.

'Just two groups then. You two with me,' Mr Gardner said, pointing to Owen and Vicky. 'Tam, you're in charge of the others.'

'Why's she in charge?' Ed demanded.

'Because she is,' Mr Gardner snapped back. 'We'll try this way. Tam, you try down there. Meet back here in ten minutes, but shout if you find anything.'

Owen's group found nothing useful. There were several telephones in offices, but none of them worked. Owen and Vicky waited outside a large room with rows of hospital beds in it. Sheets were pulled up over what Owen supposed were blankets and pillows underneath. Mr Gardner checked under the sheets.

'What is?' Vicky asked.

Mr Gardner seemed angry when he came out of the room. 'Nothing,' he said sharply. 'Nothing at all.'

A few minutes later, they were all back together in the main corridor.

'There's a door at the end of the corridor,' Tam told them. 'It's been smashed open, like the front doors. Inside there're steps down, but we didn't have time to look.'

'And Mikey was scared,' Ed added, grinning.

'Was not,' Mikey protested.

'We'll all go and look,' Mr Gardner decided. 'There's nothing much more to see up here.'

From somewhere outside came a roar. It tailed off into a growl.

'The wind?' Ed said. It certainly didn't sound like it.

'Who's scared now?' Mikey asked.

'All of us,' Tam told him. 'And with good reason. People are *dead*.'

Wide concrete steps led down from the shattered remains of the door at the end of the corridor.

'I don't like this,' Vicky complained as they started down.

'None of us like it,' Ed told her. 'So belt up.'

'Thank you, Ed,' Mr Gardner said.

A chilly breeze was blowing up from wherever the stairs led. It brought with it a strange, musty smell that would have been more in keeping with warm air. There was light, but it was of a strange quality – not exactly flickering, but sort of uneven. When they reached the bottom of the stairs, Owen could see why.

The steps ended in a huge, open area like an aircraft hangar. At the far end, enormous double doors had been bent open, torn back like the foil top of a yoghurt pot. The metal creaked and groaned in the wind that was blowing snow in. That was why the light seemed odd. The daylight from outside mingled with the red emergency lights, and the bright light reflected off the snow but seemed to flicker as more snow was blown in.

One side of the enormous area was separated from the rest by large metal bars like a cage. A section in the middle was open where a wide gate had been slid aside. On the other side of the bars, the floor was scattered with straw. Owen didn't look too closely, but he could see what looked like a dead sheep lying in the straw.

'That's gross!' Vicky had seen it too.

But the others were already walking quickly in the opposite direction. Towards the dead bodies.

Partly covered by the blown snow, there were three of them. The bodies of a man and a woman, both wearing white lab coats, lay not far from the bottom of the stairs. The woman was facing back towards the stairs, sprawled as if she'd been running towards them. Her right hand was stretched out, like she was reaching for help. The man was spread-eagled nearby. His lab coat was ripped and torn, and Owen thought Ed was right – something had been feeding on the bodies.

Further away lay the body of another man. His fair hair was stained dark and he was missing an arm.
Owen swallowed.

'What did this?' Tam gasped, looking around in horror.

Her expression was mirrored on all their faces as from outside the broken doors came the roaring sound again. It was closer this time – unmistakably an animal.

'I don't know,' Mr Gardner said. 'But whatever it was, it's still around.'

Chapter 6

The roar came again from outside, cutting through the snowy air. They all retreated to the steps, hurrying back up to the main corridor.

'There has to be some way of contacting the mainland,' Ed said. 'We need to get help.' He sounded scared.

'There's no mobile-phone signal,' Mr Gardner told him. 'And the landlines are out. There's no power even. That's why the emergency lights are on.'

'I don't think they'd get power from the mainland. They must have a generator,' Owen said.

'Oh, you'd know all about it then, would you?' Ed snapped.

'No,' Owen admitted. 'I was just saying.'

'Well, don't!'

'That's enough,' Mr Gardner said sharply. 'He's probably right. The emergency lights must run on a backup generator, so there's no knowing how long they'll last. But at least here we're under cover and out of the blizzard.'

'Didn't help those people we found,' Mikey said. He sounded angry and scared at the same time. 'Probably didn't help Brendan or Jude either. It won't help us either – none of us is getting out of this place alive, are we?'

'Enough!' Mr Gardner insisted. 'You're not helping, Mikey. Not helping at all.'

Beside Owen, Vicky was sniffing and he could tell she was trying not to cry. He felt like crying himself, but he knew it wouldn't do any good. He shuddered to think what Ed would say. The way the boy glared at him and Vicky scared Owen almost as much as whatever was outside. Almost.

'Batteries …,' Tam said thoughtfully. 'There was a computer in one of the rooms we looked in.'

'Duh – no power, remember?' Ed said.

'It was a laptop,' Mikey told him.

'So?'

'So maybe the battery's charged,' Owen realised.

'Maybe he does know something after all,' Tam told Ed.

'Show us, Tam,' Mr Gardner said. 'It's worth a try.'

Tam led them down the corridor to an office. Unlike some of the other rooms, this one was intact. It looked as if someone had only just left – there was even a cold mug of coffee beside the laptop on the desk.

'Any chance the email's working?' Mr Gardner asked as Tam sat at the desk and tried the computer.

'No. The network needs power. And if this laptop was on when the power went off, it might have drained the battery. Unless …'

Owen leaned forward to see the screen. As he watched, it flared into life, becoming the brightest source of light in the red-glow of the emergency lighting.

'Still some power in it then,' Mr Gardner said.

'Not much,' Tam told them. 'It must have gone into sleep mode. That saves a lot of energy, but it does still drain the battery.'

'How long will it last?' Owen asked.

'Half an hour, if we're lucky.'

'What good is it anyway?' Ed demanded. 'We can't send an email.'

'Maybe we can find out what happened here,' Mikey said. He seemed calmer now, after his outburst earlier.

'Or discover what they were working on,' Owen added.

'How's that help?' Vicky asked.

'No idea,' Owen told her.

'Oh, great.'

Tam was working away at the keyboard and mouse. 'Network's dead,' she told them. 'Most of the files are encrypted. I can get into them, but it will take time.'

Owen could see a set of folders arranged along the edge of the desktop screen. They had names like 'Gene Listings' and 'Clone Tissue'. One was called 'Test Subjects'. He leaned across and pointed at it. 'What's that?'

Tam opened the folder. The files inside all had a graphic of a small key over the bottom corner to show they were locked and coded. 'Names of people,' she said, reading off some of them. 'David Barnham, Razz Choslik, Maggie Fisher, Katie Mendes, Dominic Napton ...'

There was a folder at the bottom of the list of files. It was named 'Gardner'.

'You a test subject, Mr Gardner?' Mikey asked, looking over Tam's shoulder.

He didn't seem amused. 'Close that up. See if you can find something useful.'

'Fat chance,' Ed grumbled.

From somewhere outside came a heavy thump. The red lights flickered.

'We should get out of here,' Mikey said. 'Before that – whatever it is – comes looking for us.'

'Don't be daft,' Mr Gardner said. 'It's just the wind, or something falling down or whatever.'

His words were almost drowned out by a loud roar that echoed down the corridor and into the office.

'Or whatever,' Tam agreed.

'It's getting closer,' Ed said. He looked very pale, even in the red light.

'I'm going to see what it is,' Mikey decided.

Like Owen, he was probably sick of just standing around, not knowing what was going on. People were dead, and they were doing nothing. Owen made to follow, but Vicky grabbed his arm.

'Are you crazy?' Vicky asked, voice trembling.

Owen didn't answer but pulled his arm free. 'We have to leave,' he said.

'And go where?' Vicky asked. Her voice was stretched out with nerves.

'Downwards,' Tam said. She pointed at the screen. 'Look – this is a map of the building. There's some sort of area sealed off underneath the big chamber with the cage bars and the doors.'

'What's down there?' Mr Gardner asked.

'No idea. Storage probably. But like the kid says, we can't stay here.'

Mikey ran back in. 'The bodies have gone!' he gasped breathlessly. 'From the corridor. Someone – some*thing*'s dragged them away.'

'How do you know?' Ed asked.

'Because they aren't there any more, that's how. There's a ... trail.'

'Unless you moved them, Ed?' Tam asked. She closed the lid of the laptop. 'I'll bring this with us. There's still a bit of juice left in it.'

'Come on, then,' Mr Gardner said. He sounded just as nervous as the rest of them.

Vicky clutched at Owen's arm again as they followed the others out of the office. 'What is it? What's out there, making that sound?'

'I don't know,' he confessed.

But his words were interrupted by another roar – louder and closer than any so far.

Tam and Mr Gardner were leading the way back towards the stairs down to the basement chamber. Mikey and Ed were close behind them, with Owen and Vicky last in line. The sound was coming from the other end of the corridor, from the reception area.

Owen glanced back that way. He wished he hadn't. Vicky's grip on his arm tightened and she gasped as she too looked back.

'Oh my –'

Ed's frightened exclamation was cut off by Mr Gardner's shout of 'Run!'

An enormous, dark shape was moving down the corridor. It almost filled the space, it was so large. Almost three metres tall, the creature reared up on its back legs, like a Tyrannosaurus. It blotted out the lights so that it seemed to be fringed with a blood-red glow. What light there was glistened on the scaly body as the creature lumbered towards them. Massive, sharp teeth glinted red.

Pale bloodshot eyes gleamed in the reptilian head as the nightmare creature opened its mouth again and roared in triumph. It leaned forward, dropping to all-fours. Claws scraped and scratched on the floor as it charged down the corridor, straight at Owen, Vicky and the others.

Chapter 7

Owen pretty much had to drag Vicky. The strength seemed to have gone out of her legs, and he yelled at her to keep running. He tried not to look back to see how close the creature was. But he could hear it pounding down the corridor. He thought he could feel its hot breath on the back of his neck.

It seemed to take forever to reach the shattered door at the end of the corridor. Owen pushed Vicky ahead of him, then dived through after her. She sprawled on the floor and glared at him. But Owen wasn't about to say sorry.

Her glare became fear and she scrambled towards the concrete steps. Everyone else was already running down them. Owen glanced over his shoulder – just in time to see a huge mouth full of massive pointed teeth coming towards him. He hurled himself out of the way.

The creature's head moved angrily from side to side. The creature itself was too big to fit through the doorway. But the metal frame was twisting and buckling as it tried to force its way in. Owen hauled Vicky to her feet and together they followed the others down into the basement.

'Guess we know what happened to those dead scientists,' Tam panted.

'What *is* that thing?' Ed asked. He sounded like a small kid rather than a teenage bully.

'Hope we never find out,' Mikey fired back.

'It's like a dinosaur,' Tam said in disbelif.

'It's the monster that farmer warned us about,' Vicky said.

'What farmer?' Mr Gardner asked.

They emerged from the bottom of the stairs into the huge, open area below the research centre.

'Just some guy,' Mikey said. 'Found us when you were looking for Brendan and Jude.'

'Guess we know what happened to them now,' Ed said.

His words were almost lost in the angry sounds from above them. The monster was still trying to force its way through.

'At least while it's up there, it can't sneak round and get through those doors,' Ed went on, pointing to where the snow was blowing in more furiously than ever.

'You're assuming there's only one of them,' Mr Gardner told him.

'Where do we go now?' Owen asked. It was obvious they wouldn't survive for long in the blizzard. Even with the coat he'd got in reception, he could feel the cold from outside biting into his bones. Beside him, Vicky was shivering.

'This way,' Tam said confidently. Of all of them, she seemed least affected by the creature's attack, and she led them to the wall opposite the cage area. 'The plan showed steps down from here.'

'There's nothing,' Ed accused.

'You mean you can't see anything,' Mr Gardner said.

Owen had been thinking the same thing, but he could just make out a rectangular outline in the scattered snow. 'Trapdoor,' he said. 'Look.' He scuffed his foot across the floor, scraping the snow away to reveal a metal trapdoor set into the ground.

'Nice one,' Mikey said.

Mr Gardner grabbed the metal ring handle on the top of the trapdoor and hauled it open. The metal protested and grated, but finally the trapdoor swung up and open.

Something sharp whipped past Owen's face. Ice, he realised. The edge of the opening was encrusted with glistening ice. Metal rungs within led downwards. They too had a sheen of ice. Owen could feel the cold from below.

'I don't like the look of that,' he said.

'Wimp,' Ed said. But his tone gave away his own fear.

'Let's just stay here,' Mikey said.

But that was no longer an option. The monstrous creature that had come after them in the corridor – or another just like it – was standing in the main doorway. It watched them across the expanse of snowy floor, then threw back its head and let out another blood-chilling roar.

'Ladies first,' Tam said. 'Come on!' She started quickly down the ladder. 'Be careful, it's slippery.'

Mr Gardner pushed Owen and Vicky in front of Ed and Mikey. 'Hurry!' he urged. He went last, pulling the trapdoor closed afterwards.

The light from above cut out as the heavy metal door clanged shut. Immediately, claws scraped across the metal. Owen felt like they were scraping down his spine as he hurried down the ladder after Vicky and Tam.

There was light, a pale otherworldly glow shining from below. It was getting even colder. Several times he almost fell, his feet or hands slipping on the iced ladder. The ice was getting thicker as they descended.

Finally, Owen heard first Tam then Vicky gasp in astonishment. A moment later, he saw why. The ladder came down into a vast cavern beneath the research station's basement. He had lost track of how long they'd been climbing or how far they must have come. But he understood now why it was so cold.

He continued down the ladder, aware of Ed's feet close above his head. If he stopped to wonder, Ed would climb down into him and maybe knock him off the ladder. So he kept going until he could jump from the ladder to stand beside Tam and Vicky on the frozen floor of the immense ice cavern.

'This place is amazing,' Tam said, struggling to keep her teeth from chattering in the cold. She shrugged off her rucksack, checking that the laptop was safe inside.

It was like a vast cave but with walls of ice. Light was getting in from somewhere, reflecting off every surface like it was polished glass. The roof curved high above them. Tunnels led into darkness, their symmetrical shape suggesting they had been deliberately cut through the ice.

'What did they do down here?' Vicky wondered.

She was right – it was obvious that the scientists had used the place for something. An area of the cavern close to the ladder had been turned into a bizarre office. There was a desk and several upright chairs. Computer screens and other equipment were all coated with a frosting of ice. Mr Gardner and the others were all looking around in amazement.

'Look at this,' Tam called from the other side of the cavern. 'This is where it came from.'

'Where what came from?' Mr Gardner asked as they all followed him to join Tam.

'The monster,' she said, pointing to the wall of ice between two of the tunnels.

As he got closer, Owen could see that part of the ice wall was darker. At first he thought it was just a shadow, a trick of the light. But then he saw that it was *inside* the ice, frozen solid. Finally, he made out the shape.

It was the same as the creature that had come after them in the research centre above. A huge reptilian head, its jaws filled to bursting with ragged teeth, stared back at him through the ice.

'They must have found that thing down here, in the caves,' Mikey said.

'And what – thawed it out?' Owen asked.

'Seems like it,' Mr Gardner agreed. 'Is it a Tyrannosaurus rex?'

'Similar,' Owen told him. 'But it has four legs instead of two. We saw it running on all fours, but a Tyrannosaurus stands upright.'

'Of course you'd know, geeky kid,' Ed said.

Owen felt himself blushing despite the cold. He did know. He found dinosaurs fascinating – but not when they were chasing after you and wanted you for dinner.

'So what is it?' Vicky asked.

'I don't know,' Owen said. 'I'm not *that* geeky. Something new maybe.'

Mr Gardner was peering closely into the ice, wiping it smooth with his gloved hand. 'I wonder where it came from. This ice can't be natural; the climate here isn't cold enough. The ice has been brought here from somewhere far colder and kept refrigerated somehow. But that creature must be dead. It must have been dead for thousands of years. If not millions of years.'

The faintest sound of the monster's angry roar filtered through from somewhere above.

'That one's not dead,' Ed said. He was shivering more than anyone, hugging himself tight against the cold. 'We're safe down here, aren't we?'

Vicky was looking at Ed. Owen saw the faintest hint of a smile as she realised how frightened the older boy really was. 'Safe?' she said. 'Depends if this one's going to wake up.'

'That's not very likely,' Mr Gardner said. But he didn't sound too sure of himself.

'Maybe not,' Tam agreed. 'But if they found it down here and somehow revived it …' She walked back to the desk, pulling out the laptop as she went.

'What do you mean?' Mikey called after her. 'I don't understand.'

Tam set the laptop down on the desk and opened the lid. 'I'm just saying, if they found that creature down here and got it out – well, they didn't carry it up the ladder, did they?'

'I suppose not,' Mikey agreed.

'So there has to be another way out of here,' Owen said. 'And,' he realised, 'another way in. Probably down one of those tunnels. A way that's big enough for that monster to get through.'

'Clever boy,' Tam said. 'Let's hope it doesn't remember the way.'

Chapter 8

'So what are we going to do?' Ed wanted to know. 'Just wait here until that monster finds us?'

'We can't go anywhere until the blizzard stops,' Mr Gardner said. 'Then we can look for help. Maybe find that farmer you met.'

'If the monster hasn't got him, like it got Brendan and Jude,' Ed said.

Tam was working at the laptop. 'I've found a folder that's not been locked,' she told them. 'It looks like some sort of project overview.'

'Oh, great,' Mikey said sarcastically. 'That'll help.'

'Knowledge is power,' Tam retorted.

'That why you hacked into that bank?' Ed asked.

Tam didn't answer. She was too busy typing. 'Got it,' she announced at last. She traced her finger down the screen as she read through the information,

Owen wasn't close enough to read it. He glanced at Vicky, and she shrugged. Owen thought she looked cold and tired, and her face was streaked with dried tears. Her jaw trembled, but he couldn't tell whether it was because she was trying not to cry or trying to keep her teeth from chattering.

'It's some sort of medical research,' Tam told them all.

'Medical?' Ed echoed.

'As far as I can tell, they found fossilised remains of one of those creatures in the Arctic somewhere and brought it here for research. They managed to salvage some DNA and cells that had been preserved in the ice.'

'And they made their own ice box?' Mikey asked.

'And we're right inside it,' Tam agreed. 'Refrigeration for the tissue they created from that original sample.'

'Cloning?' Mr Gardner asked.

Tam nodded. 'They grew a whole new creature from a few surviving cells from that first creature's remains and recreated the DNA pattern. It was incubated inside the ice down here and automatically fed doses of sedative and food until it was fully grown. Then they woke it up. Like being born, only millions of years late. And, from what we've seen so far, they kept it in the cage up in that basement area.'

'Except it got out somehow. But why do it?' Owen asked. 'I don't see what it's got to do with medicine.'

'It seems the cell structure of these creatures is rather strange,' Tam went on, reading rapidly down the screen. 'It's resistant to all sorts of diseases. The plan is to experiment on them, take tissue samples and develop cures. They were doing tests to find out how to transfer the right genes and cell proteins to human tissue. The only problem is …' She tailed off and said nothing as she scrolled down the window.

'Yes?' Ed prompted.

When she looked up from the computer, Tam looked afraid. Owen realised it was the first time he'd seen her at all worried. Of them all, including Mr Gardner, Tam was the calm, unflustered one. What could have frightened her now?

'They need *living* cell tissue. They need large samples of cell tissue to try to transfer the genes between species. And not just to experiment on; they need human tissue to grow the new creatures.'

'So?' Mikey said.

'So, they get it from what they call "donors".'

'What – like giving blood?' Vicky asked.

'Only I don't think this is voluntary,' Tam said. 'And I don't think the donor survives the process.' As she said it, the laptop's screen went blank. 'That's it – battery's dead.'

There was a heavy silence in the icy chamber as everything that Tam had said sunk in. Had the scientists here really been experimenting on people? Owen found it hard to believe. Even harder that the 'donors' didn't live to benefit from the research or to tell the tale. But the evidence was all around them. However unpleasant, it had to be true. From the way everyone else looked, he guessed they felt the same.

Finally, Mr Gardner clapped his hands together. His breath was a misty cloud in the cold air. 'Right then, we need to find another way out of here. There must be one, like Tam said. If they grew that creature down here, they didn't get it out up that ladder.'

'So we find a way out, then what?' Mikey asked.

'Then we wait for the blizzard to ease and get back to the harbour. See if our boat survived.'

'I bet it didn't,' Ed said.

'What about my uncle?' Vicky demanded.

Owen felt guilty; he'd completely forgotten about Uncle Andy. Maybe he'd recovered and somehow managed to send for help. 'We can collect him on the way. I'm sure he just had a bump on the head,' he assured Vicky. 'He'll be OK.'

'Let's split into groups and see if we can find the way out.'

They separated into two groups, one to try each of the two largest tunnels. Mr Gardner was with Ed and Mikey, while Tam was put in charge of Owen and Vicky.

'Great,' she said, sighing. 'I get the babies. You can stay here if you want while I try the tunnel.'

Owen was disappointed by her attitude and was tempted to agree to stay in the huge ice cavern.

But Vicky was obviously also annoyed and was determined to prove she wasn't a baby. 'We'll come with you. You might need help.'

Tam raised her eyebrows but didn't object. Without comment, she led them into the third tunnel. The walls were smooth and slick. It was so regular and even that the tunnel must have been made deliberately, cut out of the ice by the scientists.

The light faded as they made their way along the tunnel. 'I don't think this is going anywhere,' Tam decided. 'We should head back.'

But Vicky held up her hand. 'No, wait. What's that noise?'

They all stopped and listened. At first, Owen couldn't hear anything. He thought Vicky must have imagined it. But then he realised that what he had mistaken for their breathing was coming from further down the tunnel. A wheezing, groaning sound – quite faint, but audible.

'Monster?' Vicky asked in a whisper.

'Baby monster if it is,' Tam said. 'We should get the others.'

'We should look for ourselves first,' Owen said. He was still annoyed that she'd called him and Vicky 'babies'.

The sound grew louder as they walked slowly forwards into the shadowy gloom. Soon they could see almost nothing as the light continued to fade. The sound grew louder.

'Who's there?' a weak and trembling voice called out.

They all stopped.

'Hello?' Tam called back.

'Who is it? Get away from me! You're not getting me back in that laboratory. Not again.'

They moved forward cautiously, and Owen could make out a dark shape huddled shivering against the icy wall of the tunnel. It was a teenage boy – about the same age as Tam. Crouching down beside him, Owen saw that, despite the cold, the boy's face was dripping with sweat.

'I'm Owen,' he said gently. 'This is Vicky and Tam.'

'Have you come to kill me?' He didn't seem to be able to focus on them, staring past Owen into the gloom.

''Course not,' Tam said.

'We want to help,' Vicky added.

'Too late. I'll be dead soon. I got away from the monster. And from the scientists. The others are all dead.'

'Dead? What others?' Tam asked.

'Found them in a room. In hospital beds, covered with sheets. All dead – Dave and Josh and Katie and Carlo. And the others. All of them.'

Owen remembered the way Mr Gardner had looked under the sheet on the bed in the room above. The way he hadn't let anyone else see what he'd found.

'What happened?' Vicky asked.

'They held us prisoner. Gave us stuff to make us sleep. Did experiments. Took skin and stuff.'

'Donors,' Tam said quietly. 'I said they weren't volunteers, remember?'

'What's your name?' Vicky asked.

'Dom.'

'We'll help you, Dom.'

'What were you doing here?' Owen asked as he and Tam tried to help the boy to his feet.

'Hiding.'

'No, I mean, here on the island. Why did you come?'

'Got into trouble.' His words were breathless gasps and he was sweating even more with the effort of standing. 'Got caught nicking stuff. They sent me away. Then they sent us here on a trip. Said it would help us adjust, learn how to behave with other people.'

His feet slipped from under him, and Dom fell to the floor with a groan. Owen looked at Tam. She was staring back at him, wide-eyed.

'Who brought you?' she asked urgently, trying to pull Dom to his feet again.

But he was too weak to help and too heavy to lift. 'Man brought us.' His voice was a hoarse whisper, getting fainter with every word. 'They knew him, the scientists did. He brings them people. Young people like me who won't be missed they said. They're right – who'll miss me?'

His eyelids fluttered then closed.

'His name,' Tam demanded. 'What's the man's name? The man who brought you here for them to experiment on – *what's his name?*'

Dom gave a last gasp. His hands clutched at Tam and Owen. Vicky stepped away, sobbing as the boy fell back, his eyes wide open and staring sightlessly up at them.

His last gasp had been painfully weak. But they'd heard what he said. They'd heard the name of the man who brought children to the research centre for the scientists to experiment on – to kill.

'Mr Gardner.'

Chapter 9

Tam bent to examine Dom.

'I'm no expert,' she admitted, 'but he's obviously dead. Poor kid.'

She closed his eyes.

'Mr Gardner,' Vicky said, her voice thick with choked-back tears. 'He really did this?'

'Better believe it,' Tam said.

But Owen found it hard to believe.

'He seemed so nice,' Vicky said quietly.

That was it – Owen had liked the man. He'd been friendly and helpful and had seemed just as shocked as the rest of them at what they'd discovered. When he'd looked under the sheets and seen the body … Had he been surprised and was keeping the awful truth from the children for their sake? Or was he keeping his crime secret?

'What do we do?' Owen wondered out loud.

Before Tam could answer, another voice called down the gloomy tunnel: 'Are you there? Tam – we think we've found a way out.'

'Mr Gardner!' Vicky exclaimed.

'We can't let him guess that we know,' Owen said quietly.

'We can't let him find Dom's body either,' Tam decided. 'We'll have to leave him here.'

'We can't,' Vicky said. 'We can't just leave him.'

But Tam was right. 'We have to,' Owen told her. He took her arm and guided her back along the tunnel.

'Are you there?' Mr Gardner called again.

'Here!' Tam called back. 'With you in a minute.'

Mr Gardner and the others were all waiting where the tunnel emerged back into the main cavern.

'Anything?' Mr Gardner asked.

'Dead end,' Tam said.

Vicky was staring at Mr Gardner, her lower lip trembling in fear and anger.

'What is it?' he asked her. 'Something wrong?'

She turned away, and Owen answered before Mr Gardner could say anything else. 'She's just cold and scared. Like the rest of us.'

Behind Mr Gardner, Tam was talking quietly and urgently to Ed and Mikey. Ed looked over at them, his expression angry. Mikey was shaking his head, as if in disbelief.

'One of the other tunnels seems to come out on the hillside below the research station,' Mr Gardner was saying, oblivious to the conversation going on behind him. 'On the other side from the lane up to the centre, so usually no one would see it.'

'But we're safe here, aren't we?' Owen asked. He glanced at Vicky. They both knew they weren't safe anywhere with this man.

'We need to find some help – not least for Vicky's uncle. Once the snow eases, we can try to find someone and get a message to the mainland. I have some friends we can call in who'll help. It'll be all right.'

The others were gathering round to listen now. Tam watched him carefully through narrowed eyes. Mikey was tense, shifting his weight from one foot to the other. Ed stared fixedly at Mr Gardner, his hands clasped behind his back.

'You had friends here too,' Tam said.

'Well, I'd hardly –' He stopped, apparently sensing the atmosphere had changed. 'Look, we should get down that tunnel and see if the snow has got any better. The further we get from here, the better.'

'You can say that again,' Mikey told him.

There was a crash from above, followed by the muffled stamping of the angry creature. It was still trying to break through to them.

'Maybe it can smell us?' Owen said.

'Maybe it can,' Tam agreed.

'What do you think, Mr Gardner?' Mikey asked. 'Can it smell us?'

'Perhaps.' He sounded puzzled and wary. 'I'm no expert.'

'Really?' Ed said.

'There's something I should tell you,' Mr Gardner said slowly. 'Something important. I should have told you earlier.'

'It's all right,' Tam said. 'We already know.'

The noise from above was getting louder. A sprinkling of ice fell from the roof and dusted Mr Gardner's shoulder. He brushed it away with his hand.

'What do you know? What are you talking about?'

'About you,' Tam said. 'We know all about you.'

'But that's not –' He broke off as more ice fell on to his shoulder and scattered across his head. He brushed it away again and glanced upwards.

Owen looked up too. There was a loud cracking sound. A whole section of the roof was breaking away, falling towards them.

'Look out!' Mr Gardner yelled.

He threw himself towards Owen and Vicky. Vicky screamed as Mr Gardner wrapped his arms round her and Owen and dragged them to the ground. Tam and the others leaped backwards as the roof crashed down.

Huge chunks of frosted ice crashed to the ground just where seconds before Owen, Vicky and Mr Gardner had been standing. They struggled to their feet.

'That was close,' Mikey said.

He and the other teenagers were also picking themselves up. Ed kicked at a large piece of ice about the size of a brick.

They all looked up again as a tremendous roar echoed round the cavern. More ice was falling, like hail. There was a ragged hole in the roof of the cavern, high above them. The scaly head of the creature was forcing its way through, staring down at them. A string of viscous saliva detached itself from the monster's jaw and splashed down close to where Ed was sifting through the chunks of fallen ice.

'Time we were going,' Mr Gardner shouted above the savage roars of the monster scrabbling through the roof.

More ice was falling. The creature had forced the upper half of its body through the roof. Soon it would fall into the cavern. Owen didn't think it would be hurt by the drop. He was sure now that the thing could scent them – it could smell food.

Mr Gardner was bending to help Vicky back to her feet. He saw something in her expression as he pulled her up. He half turned to see what it was.

But he was too late.

Ed brought the heavy chunk of ice crashing down on the back of Mr Gardner's head. The man grunted in surprise and pain and fell to the floor. Vicky's hands were over her mouth in shock.

'What are you doing?' Owen gasped.

'What do you think? I'm not giving him a chance to sell us out.'

'We're all in this together right now,' Owen said. 'We needed him. He must know about that monster. He might know how to escape from it, even how to kill it.'

'The kid's right,' Tam told Ed. 'That was stupid.'

'Is he dead?' Vicky asked in a small voice.

'Who cares?' Ed told her. 'Let's just get out of here.'

'He's just knocked out,' Tam said, examining Mr Gardner. 'He's breathing.'

'Just leave him,' Ed said. 'Let's get out of here.'

Another section of the roof was falling, crashing across the ground and making them all leap out of the way.

'We can't leave him here,' Owen said.

'Why not?' Mikey asked.

'I can,' Ed said.

'We don't have a lot of choice,' Tam told Owen. 'Unless you want to carry him.'

But there was no time even to answer. With a roar of triumph, the monster forced its way right through the widening hole in the roof. More ice smashed down, and the creature was coming with it. Its feet thumped into the ground, sending dark cracks out like a spider's web across the icy floor. Its tail lashed out, sending the desk flying. Through a storm of falling ice crystals, it roared again and turned its bloodshot eyes towards Owen and Vicky and the others.

Chapter 10

The monster had landed in the middle of the ice cavern, cutting off any chance Owen and the others had of getting to any of the tunnels except the one where they had found Dom. And that tunnel was a dead end. If they went into it, they'd be trapped.

'Split up,' Tam said. 'See if we can edge past it and get to the tunnels.'

'We can't just leave Mr Gardner,' Vicky said.

'Sure we can,' Ed told her. 'He was planning on getting us killed. Look what he did to Bren and Jude.'

'We don't know he did anything,' Mikey told him.

'That's what Dom said,' Owen said.

'Some dead kid.'

'We'll all be dead kids soon,' Tam pointed out.

They were all backing away as the monster stood watching them. Its head swayed back and forth as if it was assessing the situation, deciding how much of a threat they might be. Not a lot, Owen thought. They didn't have anything that could be used as a weapon, and there was very little cover in the cavern. So why didn't it just attack them?

'What's it hanging about for?' Ed whispered.

'Don't worry about it hearing you,' Tam told him. 'It's looking right at us.'

But was it? Owen turned to check what was behind them. What might be holding the creature back. But it was just the shiny ice of the cavern wall. Like a mirror, it reflected back Owen's frightened face – the curve of the wall magnifying his features like a fairground mirror.

'That's it,' he realised.

'What are you talking about?' Vicky asked. 'What's it?'

'The monster's not looking at us. It can see its own reflection.' The monster's refection was also magnified and distorted. 'It doesn't recognise itself, and it's scared of what looks like another monster.'

'It can join the club,' Mikey said. 'We're all scared.'

'Slowly then,' Tam told them. 'Let's see if we can edge past it while it's distracted.'

The creature's hot breath was steaming out of its nostrils. It reared up, front feet clawing at the air. The claws on its back feet scraped across the ice. It leaned forwards, slamming down on to all four feet again.

Owen realised the monster was about to charge. It pawed the ground like an impatient horse, gathering itself ready to attack.

'Look out,' he yelled.

But the creature was already hurtling towards them. Ice kicked up like mist around its feet as it charged. The children scattered both ways. The monster kept coming –

heading straight for its own reflection, which seemed to be charging back towards it.

With an angry bellow, the monster lowered its head and slammed straight into the wall of ice. The wall cracked and crazed. Ice showered down. The monster slumped to the ground, breathing heavily.

'Let's hope it's killed itself,' Ed said.

'No chance,' Tam told him. 'Look.'

The monster was already getting groggily back to its feet. It shuffled and lurched in confusion.

'Its reflection's gone,' Vicky said.

The wall was a mess of cracks and craters, reflecting nothing but scattered light.

'It'll look for something else to attack now,' Owen realised.

'No prizes for guessing what,' Tam agreed.

They all edged slowly round the outside of the cavern. In the middle of the ice cave lay the unconscious body of Mr Gardner. He'd been lucky to escape being trampled by the rampaging monster. Whatever Owen felt about the man, there was no way they could get to him now. They would be lucky if they could save themselves.

The creature was turning back and forth, sniffing the air. Owen wondered if it hunted by sight or smell. Probably both, he decided as it fixed its terrible eyes on him.

'Keep going,' Vicky urged, and Owen realised he'd stopped when the monster looked at him.

'Which tunnel?' Tam asked, her voice a hushed whisper.

'The far one,' Mikey told her. 'Of course.'

'Great.'

The monster swayed on its feet. Again, its claws scraped at the frozen ground as it prepared to attack. What was keeping it from charging this time? The other walls of the cavern were not so smooth, and they didn't reflect the monster.

Except, Owen saw, the wall between the two tunnels was where the other monster was embedded, frozen and preserved.

'It's just as scared of the dead one as it is of its reflection,' he said. 'Keep going.'

They passed the first tunnel, and still the monster did not attack. Owen dared to think that they might actually make it.

The sound of ice cracking made Owen look up again. He thought that more of the roof was about to come down. But then he realised the sound wasn't coming from above but from behind him. He heard Vicky give a gasp of fear. Ed swore. Mikey caught his breath and stared in horror.

Slowly, Owen turned to see what they were looking at. He was aware of Tam turning as well.

'They were born down here, remember?' she said.

Owen did remember. 'Fed sedatives until it was time to wake. But now,' he said, the awful truth washing over him like cold water, 'the power's off.'

'So the sedatives have stopped,' Mikey said.

'And it's waking up,' Vicky realised.

Another crack of ice. The creature inside the wall stared back at them through red-rimmed eyes. The scales on its head looked slick and wet – as if the ice round it was thawing. Melting.

A claw twitched. A leg moved, just slightly. The head turned, just enough for Owen to be sure the monster frozen in the wall was looking at him.

Then the whole wall cracked open. Ice showered down as the wall shattered like glass. A clawed, reptilian leg kicked out. A tail smashed its way through ice and slush. The monster in the wall thrashed and fought, struggling out of its icy prison. Its muffled roars became clearer and louder as it broke free.

From across the cavern came an answering roar. The other monster reared up on its hind legs.

'Run!' Tam yelled.

And both creatures charged towards them.

Chapter 11

For a moment, they all stood frozen in fear and unable to move.

'Run!' Tam yelled again.

She was the first to move, diving aside as the monster from the cavern wall thundered towards her. She dragged Mikey with her. Ed scrambled after them. Owen pulled Vicky clear as the monster charged past.

Owen's feet slipped on the icy ground, and they both fell – just as a massive claw slashed through the air above them. Owen rolled desperately out of the way as the creature's foot slammed down, cracking the iced floor where he'd just been lying. Someone grabbed his hand and helped him struggle out of the way – it was Vicky.

The two creatures had stopped and were eyeing each other warily. They paced round each other, like some lumbering dance of the dinosaurs.

Beyond the creatures, Tam and the others stood in the mouth of the tunnel.

'Come on!' Mikey shouted. 'Don't just stand there.'

'Get going,' Owen shouted back. 'We'll follow.'

'If we can get past those things,' Vicky added.

The monsters had turned, hearing Mikey call out. Their snorts of anger misted the air.

'We need to distract them,' Owen said. 'Or else they'll follow Tam and the others.'

'Distract them – are you mad?'

'Maybe,' Owen admitted.

But the distraction came from somewhere else. In the centre of the cavern, Mr Gardner was struggling to his feet. He rubbed the back of his head, swaying groggily.

'What happened? Where – *Hello?*' he called.

Then he saw the two creatures turning slowly towards him.

'Look out!' Vicky shouted.

Perhaps they thought the injured man was easier prey than the others. Or perhaps they could smell the blood from the wound on Mr Gardner's head where Ed had hit him with the chunk of ice. But for whatever reason, the creatures ignored Vicky and Owen. They stalked slowly and heavily towards Mr Gardner, feet thumping down on to the ice. The whole cavern shook, ice sprinkling down from the shattered roof.

Mr Gardner backed away. 'You two get out of here,' he shouted to Owen and Vicky. 'Find Tam and the others. Save yourselves.'

'What do you care about us?' Owen shouted back. He knew the monsters might hear, might turn to attack him and Vicky. But he couldn't help his anger at the man. 'You were going to get them all killed anyway. Us too.'

Mr Gardner shook his head. 'No, that's not true.'

'You were working with the scientists,' Vicky shouted. 'Dom told us.'

'Who?'

'Just a boy,' Owen said. 'And he's dead now – thanks to you.'

'I didn't – I never …' Mr Gardner started to reply.

But then the monsters both quickened their pace, sensing perhaps that their prey was distracted.

'Just get out of here!' Mr Gardner shouted above the sound of cracking ice and pounding feet. Then he turned and ran for the other tunnel.

'It's a dead end,' Owen said. 'He'll be trapped in there.'

'You want to help him?' Vicky asked.

Owen shrugged. He just didn't know. The man had intended to get them all killed. But could they just abandon him to the monsters?

'There's nothing we can do anyway,' Vicky pointed out.

She took Owen's hand, and he was surprised how gently she held it. He was also surprised at how she looked sad rather than frightened.

'Come on,' she said.

They ran down the tunnel. The sounds of the monsters grew fainter behind them. The light that illuminated the cavern seemed to be coming from the end of the tunnel. They ran towards it.

Water dripped from the roof of the tunnel. A drop splashed on Owen's bare neck, making him yelp with surprise at the sudden cold. The ground became more like slush as the air got noticeably warmer. Whatever freezing system had been used was failing now. The whole place was thawing out.

'Nearly there,' he told Vicky.

Several figures were silhouetted in the mouth of the tunnel. The ice was all gone here, and the tunnel was rock and earth.

'Thought you weren't coming,' Tam said when they reached the end of the tunnel.

'What did you do with the monsters?' Mikey asked.

There was a rumbling roar from behind them, as if in answer.

'They went after Mr Gardner,' Vicky said.

Ed smiled. 'Good. I hope they eat him.'

There was another roar – closer now and echoing down the tunnel.

'I think they've finished dinner,' Mikey said. 'And I can guess what's for afters.'

The snow had stopped and the evening was bright but cloudy. The tunnel emerged from the side of a hill. Owen guessed the research station was on top of the hill. Below them, snowy moorland stretched into the distance. Long grass poked out through the snow and rippled in the wind.

'Let's not hang about,' Owen decided. 'We need to find someone and get a message out for help.'

'Or get back to the boat,' Tam said. 'Though it's probably smashed to bits after that storm.'

'We need to find my uncle,' Vicky told them.

'We need to get as far away from here as possible,' Ed said.

'That's right,' Vicky snapped. 'You think about yourself before anyone else.'

Ed leaned forward, his face close to Vicky's. 'I will. So don't you get in my way.'

Vicky held his gaze for a moment, then she looked away.

'Come on, then,' Tam said, leading the way down the hill.

It was hard going. The grass was long and wet, and the ground was covered in snow and soft under foot. Although the snow had all but stopped, the air was damp, and Owen felt it seeping into his clothes.

They walked in silence. The evening was drawing in, the sun dipping towards the horizon in front of them. Owen wondered how long it had been since he was on Vicky's uncle's boat thinking that things couldn't get any worse. If only he'd known.

Their shadows stretched out behind them across the moorland. In other circumstances, Owen thought it would have been a pleasant walk.

'This is about the best weather we've had the whole time we've been here,' Mikey said. 'Maybe things are looking up at last.'

'Not for Jude and Brendan and all those other kids,' Tam snapped.

They walked on in gloomy silence for a few minutes. Then Tam said, 'Hey, I'm sorry, Mikey.'

He smiled weakly. 'You're right though. Jude was all right. So was Bren.'

They were approaching a small cluster of trees on top of a low hill when a distant bellow made them all turn.

'Is it coming this way?' Owen wondered.

'Following our scent, maybe,' Tam said. 'We should keep moving.'

There was another sound, from off to their side, like the rustling of long grass only louder.

'They've split up,' Mikey realised.

'At least we know they're still behind us,' Ed said.

Even though the slope was gentle, climbing the hill was an effort. Owen's feet seemed to stick in the ground, like a nightmare. But he didn't complain – if Vicky could do it, so could he. She walked with her head down, saying nothing. But Owen could see that inside her coat she was shivering.

'We'll rest for a bit once we get to the trees,' Tam said.

'Who put you in charge?' Ed demanded.

'All right, what's your plan?'

'I need a rest,' Mikey said. 'And once we're in the trees we'll have some shelter. From the top we can probably see all the way back to the research centre.'

'Might be able to see where those creatures have got to,' Owen said.

'I don't want to know,' Vicky muttered.

It was further than it looked, and by the time they reached the trees it was getting dark. Mikey and Tam still had their rucksacks, and they slipped them off. Tam took a bar of chocolate out of hers and broke it into squares, which she handed round. Owen had not realised how hungry he was until he put the chocolate into his mouth. Mikey had a water bottle, and they all took sips.

'Do we spend the night here, Tam?' Ed asked.

'Who put me in charge?' she asked him.

'At least there's shelter,' Vicky said.

'What do you think, Mikey?' Tam said.

There was no reply.

'Mikey?'

'Shhh!' Mikey was standing slightly away from the rest of them, further into the trees.

'What?' Owen asked in a whisper.

In answer, Mikey pointed deeper into the small wood. 'I can hear something. Over there.'

They all held their breath and listened. Mikey was right, there was something. Like the sighing of the wind in the trees, or perhaps the purring of a giant cat.

'Oh, it's nothing,' Ed said. 'You're imagining things. It's just the wind.'

'I don't think so,' Tam said slowly.

The purring became a rumble of noise. A huge, dark shape reared up among the trees in front of them. Red eyes glinted in the remaining light. Massive, sharp teeth gleamed as they caught the dying rays of the sun.

Chapter 12

They all backed slowly away.

'You said they were behind us,' Vicky said in a trembling voice.

'They were,' Tam replied quietly.

'There must be three of the creatures,' Owen realised.

The ugly reptilian head turned slowly towards them.

Owen's foot caught on a fallen branch and he stumbled. Vicky caught his arm.

The monster stalked towards them, pushing smaller trees out of its way and snapping branches.

'If it gets us in the open, we've had it,' Mikey said. 'It's got to be faster than we are.'

'We should split up,' Ed said.

'And hope it gets someone else and not you?' Tam asked.

'It can't chase us all. I was just saying.'

'Well, don't.'

They backed out of the trees. Mikey was right, Owen thought. It was hard enough walking through the long, wet, snowy grass. Running would be almost impossible. They'd never get any speed, and they'd probably fall down, the ground was so uneven. Maybe Ed had a point.

'Keep going slowly,' Owen said. 'Maybe something will distract it.'

'Like what?' Tam asked. 'You expecting a group of jugglers or a party clown?'

The monster lumbered out of the wood and stared down at the retreating figures. It threw its head back and let out an almighty bellow of sound. Somewhere in the distance, other roars answered.

'Oh, great,' Tam muttered. 'Now they're calling a meeting to discuss the menu.'

'Don't joke!' Ed snapped. 'It's not funny. None of this is funny.'

Ed was trembling. His face was pale in the fading light and his eyes were wide. The teenager who seemed so hard and unforgiving was really frightened. Before Owen could say anything, Ed turned and ran.

Immediately the monster was after him. It hurtled down the hill, roaring in triumph. Ed turned to look over his shoulder, but he tripped and went headlong. The monster was standing over him, looking down. Saliva dripped from its hungry jaws.

'We've got to help him,' Vicky said.

'Have we?' Mikey asked.

The rest of them were saved from answering by a sudden flash of light in the trees. A moment later, a ball of fire exploded against the creature's flank. It roared in pain, flames licking up its body. The monster staggered back. Its long tail lashed out, just missing Ed, who was cowering on the ground. The flames were dying down, but the monster was still roaring in pain as it stumbled quickly away as if trying to outrun the fire.

'What was *that*?' Vicky gasped.

A dark shape detached itself from the trees and walked purposefully down towards them. As he got closer, Owen saw that it was the farmer who had spoken to them earlier. He had a shotgun slung over his shoulder and was holding what looked like a short, stubby pistol.

'I didn't reckon this would do much good against that thing,' he said, patting the shotgun. 'So I used the flare gun. Seemed to do the trick, for now at least.'

The monster's roars of pain still echoed through the twilight.

'Thank you,' Tam said. The others all added their thanks, including Ed who had staggered up to join them. He was covered in mud and sounded rather subdued.

'You'd best come with me, before that thing comes back with its friends.'

The farmer led them back through the woods. On the other side of the hill, the marshland became fields. Nestling at the bottom of the hill was a small stone-built farmhouse. Smoke was curling up from the chimney and there were lights on inside.

'You don't seem to be surprised to find monsters roaming round your farm,' Owen said as they approached the house.

'Nothing much surprises me any more. What they get up to at that research station ...' He shrugged.

'We need to send for help, from the mainland,' Tam said. 'Those monsters have killed everyone up there.'

The farmer nodded. 'I know.'

He opened the door and gestured for them to go inside. The door opened straight into a small living room. A narrow flight of steps led up from the side of the room. There was a fire burning, and they all gathered round it, grateful for the warmth.

'Do you have a phone?' Tam asked.

'I do.' The farmer slipped the shotgun off his shoulder and held it loosely, pointing it at the floor.

'Have you called for help?' Vicky asked. 'There might be people who are just injured, and my uncle –'

The farmer cut her off. 'I haven't called for help. And I'm sorry to say I'm not going to.'

They all turned in surprise. The man's voice had hardened. He raised the shotgun so it was pointing right at them.

'He's in it with them,' Tam said quietly. 'Aren't you? In with the scientists and Mr Gardner.'

'I meant to ask you,' the farmer said. 'What's happened to Gardner?'

'The monsters got him,' Owen said. He was pretty sure that was true, even if he and Vicky hadn't actually seen it happen.

The farmer sniffed. 'Pity. He was clever and efficient.

He said he was bringing five kids on a certain date and you knew he'd do it. Very reliable.'

'What about you?' Mikey asked.

'I'm reliable too.' He jabbed the gun forward as Ed stepped towards him. 'Don't try it, lad. The shot from this will cut you in two. Probably kill a few more of you in the process.'

Ed stepped back, as the farmer went on. 'Yes, Mr Gardner brings the kids. I keep watch and let the scientists know if anyone else comes to the island. I keep the boss informed of progress.'

'The boss?' Owen asked. He couldn't take his eyes off the shotgun.

'He owns the company that runs the research station. He doesn't come here often, but he likes to be kept up to date.'

'Shame we won't meet him then,' Tam said.

The farmer laughed. It was a thin, cruel sound. 'I said he doesn't come here often, but he's here now. In fact, he's looking forward to meeting you. After all, you're the batch of organic material he needs to restart the experiments.'

Someone was coming down the stairs. A dark figure that emerged slowly into the flickering light cast by the fire. The man responsible for the research station, for the terrible experiments, the dead children and the monsters. It was a man that Owen recognised.

Beside him, Vicky gasped in astonishment. 'Uncle Andy!'

Chapter 13

'Leave these two with me,' Uncle Andy said, nodding at Owen and Vicky. 'Lock the others up somewhere.'

'The barn's secure enough,' the farmer said. 'They won't get out of there.'

Owen watched, helpless and disbelieving, as the farmer led Tam, Mikey and Ed out of the farmhouse. Only Ed objected, but a swift blow to the head from the butt of the farmer's shotgun shut him up.

'What's going on?' Vicky demanded as soon as she and Owen were alone with Uncle Andy.

'Just business,' he replied. He sat down in a small, threadbare armchair close to the fire and warmed his hands.

'*Business?*' Vicky snapped.

Owen did not trust himself to say anything. Inside, he was boiling with anger. This man, whose hospitality he'd accepted, even if he hadn't really enjoyed it, was responsible for the monsters and for the deaths. Now he was locking up the others.

'Please don't shout,' Uncle Andy said, his tone calm and reasonable. 'I feel a lot better for a short rest, but my head is still rather delicate. Thank you for getting me to shore, by the way. And leaving your lifejackets and phones was a clever way of letting me know you were all right. I guessed you'd gone for help. Thanks for that too, but McLaren, the farmer, found me.'

Vicky started to reply, her face pale with anger. But Uncle Andy cut her off.

'I know, I know. People have died. Terrible things have happened. The project creatures are on the loose. But it's all under control, I promise you. As soon as I can get them here, I'll have a team of experts clear up the mess. Together with McLaren and Gardner, if he's still with us, they can recapture the creatures. Then we can pick up where we were forced to leave off with the new batch of experimental material waiting in the barn.'

By 'experimental material', he meant Tam and the others. Owen could see from Vicky's expression that she had realised that too.

'So,' Uncle Andy went on, 'the only real problem is what to do about you two?'

'About us?' Owen said. He was surprised how calm he sounded. He knew they were in a terribly dangerous situation.

'My charming new niece and her rather common and ungrateful cousin. So, are you going to see reason, or will I have to send you both out to join the others in the barn? Just another experiment waiting to happen?'

'See reason?' Vicky echoed in disbelief. 'What you're doing – the experiments – it's *wrong*.'

'Oh, come on.' Uncle Andy sounded almost bored. 'You're just children; you don't understand.'

'People have died,' Owen told him. 'What's to understand? Vicky's right. It's monstrous.'

'Interesting choice of word,' Uncle Andy said. 'But you're not seeing the big picture. So what if a few unwanted kids have to die? Runaways and young offenders. They're no use to anyone. No one's going to miss them.'

'They're still *people*,' Vicky said.

'Barely. At least this way they're doing some good; they're helping society. At least this way their lives will have meant something. If a dozen or so cheap deaths result in research that develops a drug that can save thousands of useful, good, law-abiding people from disease, then isn't it worth it?'

Neither Vicky nor Owen replied. Owen could tell there was no point in arguing. The man wasn't suddenly going to see sense and let them go. If they said the wrong thing, they would be in the barn and after that …

'I'll give you a few minutes to think about it while I talk to McLaren about getting a message to my people in Glasgow,' Uncle Andy said. 'It's your choice, and it's a very easy one. You see things my way, or you get to help with the experiments in a more direct manner. I'm sure you take my point.'

'You mean, we keep quiet or we die,' Owen said.

Uncle Andy stood up and smiled. 'I told you it was easy. I'll give you ten minutes, then you have to decide.'

Uncle Andy closed the door behind him. They both heard the unmistakable sound of a key turning in the lock.

'What do you think?' Owen asked.

'I think he's more of a monster than those things out there,' Vicky said. 'But I don't want to die.'

'I don't want anyone to die,' Owen said.

'What do you think we should do?'

'There's only one thing we can do,' Owen said. He didn't even have to think about it. 'Get out of here and rescue the others from the barn before your uncle and McLaren kill them – or worse. Then we have to get off this island and tell people what's been going on.'

'Will anyone believe us?'

'We have to try. Maybe the children really haven't been missed, but once people start asking and looking …'

'And the dead scientists,' Vicky agreed. 'They must have families and friends, people who will wonder what's happened to them. But how do we get out of here? He locked the door.'

Owen nodded. 'Our advantage is that he thinks we're frightened kids who'll go along with what he says because we're scared. And because he's a grown-up, we'll think he must be right. He'll expect us to wait here, probably crying our eyes out, and play nicely.'

Vicky nodded and sniffed. Owen could see that she was about ready to cry, and he knew that wouldn't help.

'There might be a back door,' Vicky suggested. 'Or if not, we can maybe get a window open and climb out.'

'Good thinking. Just so long as we avoid McLaren's shotgun.' Owen forced a smile, which he hoped reassured

Vicky. 'Come on, then. He gave us ten minutes to decide, then he'll be back for us.'

The windows in the living room were quite small. It would take them ages to squeeze through. The biggest window was by the front door, and they would probably be seen. Another door led from the small living room out to a tiny kitchen with a stone-tiled floor. There was a third door that probably led outside, but it was locked.

Over the sink and draining board was a window. It was a bit larger than the ones in the living room, and Owen reckoned they could fit through. He climbed up on to the drainer. The window was stiff, and it creaked when he finally managed to shove it open. He froze, listening for a shout from outside, or running footsteps. Or a gunshot.

But there was nothing apart from the whine of the wind.

'Hurry up,' Vicky hissed.

Owen turned round awkwardly so he could push his legs out of the window first, then levered the rest of his body through. What Owen had thought was a ledge turned out to be a large rectangular metal tank. It clanged as his feet bumped against it. Taking care to make no more noise,

Owen crawled to the edge and dropped to the ground. It was slippery with mud and he almost fell.

A moment later, Vicky followed. She leaned over from the top of the tank to see where Owen was. He reached up and helped her down.

'Thanks. This tank must be full of heating oil. It was quite warm in there, even with the fire burning.' She smiled.

Owen couldn't remember when she'd last smiled. He realised he was smiling back. 'Let's find the barn and let the others out,' he said.

It had got properly dark since they arrived at the farmhouse. There were dark shapes in the distance, but it was impossible to tell what they were. They headed for the largest, darkest shape. As they got closer, it resolved itself into a large windowless building.

'This must be it,' Vicky said. 'How do we get in?'

'We don't want to get in; we want to get the others *out*.'

They followed the wall of the barn, hoping to find a door. But they reached the corner without any success.

As they turned the corner, a shape detached itself from the wall ahead. A sudden shaft of moonlight cut through the clouds and revealed the figure walking towards them. His coat was torn and there was blood streaked down his face.

'Just who I was looking for,' Mr Gardner said.

Chapter 14

Owen and Vicky backed away.

'We thought you were dead, Mr Gardner,' Owen said. He wondered if they could run for it. But he doubted Vicky was strong or fast enough to get away. He wasn't sure *he* was.

'I thought I was dead too,' Mr Gardner replied. 'But I managed to get to the tunnel, and it was too narrow for those creatures to follow. They scrabbled about for a bit, then gave up.'

'They came after us,' Vicky said. 'And another one.'

'In the tunnel,' Mr Gardner said, 'I found a boy …'

'Dom,' Vicky said. 'His name was Dom.'

Mr Gardner nodded. If he hadn't known better, Owen might have thought he was sad. 'Poor lad,' he murmured.

'You say that like it wasn't your fault,' Owen said. 'Like you didn't trick him into going to the research station – him and all the others. You might as well have murdered Dom and the others yourself.'

Mr Gardner was shaking his head.

'Dom told us,' Vicky said. 'We know all about what you've been up to. He said it was you that took him and his friends to the research centre and handed them over to the scientists to experiment on.'

'He knew your name,' Owen agreed. 'We didn't ask. He said it was Mr Gardner. You going to tell us he was wrong?'

'No, of course not. But what you don't realise –'

'Why did you do it?' Vicky interrupted loudly. 'Money was it? I bet that's it. Greed. Uncle Andy has lots of money.'

'Who?' Mr Gardner asked.

'She means me. Vicky is my niece. Or, rather, my sister's stepdaughter.'

Owen hadn't seen or heard the other figure arrive until he stepped out into the pale moonlight.

'Andrew Lawrence,' Uncle Andy introduced himself. 'We've communicated so many times, and you've done such a lot of very good work for us. It's a delight finally to meet you, Mr Gardner.'

To Owen's astonishment, they actually shook hands. Like they were just two business colleagues meeting. But then, he supposed, they were – to them the experiments and the lives of the young people they snuffed out were just business. Vicky was right. It all came down to money.

But then Mr Gardner looked sideways at Owen and Vicky. And he winked. What did that mean? Was he gloating now they were prisoners again?

'We'll lock these two in the barn with the others,' Uncle Andy said. 'Since they seem to have made up their minds not to be helpful.'

'I'll do that,' Mr Gardner said. 'Don't worry, they won't give me any trouble.'

'That's what you think,' Vicky snapped. Mr Gardner ignored her.

'It's all right,' Uncle Andy said. 'McLaren can do it.'

'McLaren?' Mr Gardner sounded wary.

'Here he is now.'

The stooped figure of the farmer stepped out of the darkness. He was holding his shotgun at the ready.

'You found them, I see,' he said to Uncle Andy.

'With a bit of help.'

'Oh?' McLaren peered at Mr Gardner.

'Of course,' Uncle Andy went on, 'you know each other quite well, don't you? How many times has Mr Gardner been to this island and enjoyed your help and hospitality after he's made his delivery, McLaren?.'

Mr Gardner shifted uncomfortably from one foot to the other.

'Must be four or five times now,' McLaren said, turning to look closely at Mr Gardner.

'No wonder you're ashamed,' Vicky said. 'How many children is that? How many have you killed?'

But McLaren and the others ignored her. McLaren raised his shotgun, pointing it directly at Mr Gardner.

'Only problem is,' the farmer said slowly, 'this man isn't David Gardner.'

'What? Then who is he?' Uncle Andy demanded.

'No idea. I've never seen him before in my life.' McLaren jabbed the shotgun towards the man who wasn't really Mr Gardner. 'Well?'

In answer, Mr Gardner turned towards Owen and Vicky. 'I never killed anyone,' he said. 'I never sent anyone to their death, certainly not children and youngsters.'

'So who are you?' snarled Uncle Andy. 'And where's Mr Gardner?'

'I believe the phrase is that he's helping the police with their enquiries.'

'*What?*' McLaren looked in alarm at Uncle Andy.

'He's bluffing,' Uncle Andy said calmly.

'No, I'm not. My name, my real name, is Will Campbell. Detective Sergeant Will Campbell. Did you really think no one would notice that the children from Mr Gardner's field trips don't come back? Oh, it took a while, I'll admit. No one's very proud about that. But the odd enquiry here, someone who seems to have vanished off the face of the earth there. It didn't take too long to trace it back and find the missing kids were all on Gardner's trips. And when we tried to find other kids from the same trips to see if they knew what had happened to the missing teenagers – guess what?'

Uncle Andy nodded. 'You found that none of them came back.'

'Exactly.'

'Except that you're bluffing.'

'I'm not.'

'Really? Then why did they just send you? Oh, I'm willing to accept there are suspicions. More information needed, I'm sure. But if the police know what *really* happened, they'd be here in force, crawling all over the island, questioning everyone connected with the research station.'

He turned in a full circle, his arms outstretched. 'Yet there's no one. No one but you, Detective Sergeant Campbell. Tell me, do any of your colleagues even know that you're here?'

The policeman didn't reply.

'They don't, do they?' Vicky said quietly to Owen. 'No one knows.'

Owen had a horrible feeling that she was right.

'Lock the children in the barn with the others,' Uncle Andy told McLaren. 'If they give you any trouble …'

'Yes?'

'Shoot them.'

From the distance came the sound of one of the monsters roaring. The answering cry was much nearer.

'You still have to deal with *them*,' the policeman said.

'I can sort them out, don't worry,' Uncle Andy told him. 'And then we'll start the experiments again. We might have to move to another island, put the police off whatever sniff of the scent they might really have got. But the creatures are no problem, not really. They belong to me.'

He smiled at Owen, Vicky and Sergeant Campbell. 'And now so do you.'

Chapter 15

There was another roar – closer this time.

'They're heading this way,' Sergeant Campbell said. 'Maybe they don't know they belong to you.'

'I've got the flare pistol and spare cartridges,' McLaren told Uncle Andy. 'That'll keep them in order. I've had a lot of practice.'

'We'll drive them back to the research station. Keep them there until my team arrive.'

While the two of them were talking, Sergeant Campbell was looking at Owen and Vicky. He moved his head slightly, which Owen realised meant they should try to slip away.

Campbell cleared his throat. As both Uncle Andy and McLaren turned towards him, Owen edged backwards, nudging Vicky to come with him.

'You'll never get away with this,' Campbell said loudly, obviously trying to keep the men's attention.

Owen and Vicky took another step back. A few more and they'd disappear into the gloom and could turn and run for it. Though Owen knew there was nowhere to go. They were on their own and stranded. Maybe, when it got light, they could somehow signal the mainland for help.

Another step backwards.

'But I have got away with it,' Uncle Andy was saying. 'It's been remarkably easy.'

'Now!' Owen whispered to Vicky.

They both turned to run.

But they were too late.

'Hold it, you two!' Uncle Andy shouted at them. 'You're not going anywhere. Except into the barn to keep your friends company.'

For a second, Owen thought of running anyway. Vicky glanced at him, and he guessed she had the same idea. But McLaren was right behind them and there was no way he could miss at this range. One blast from his shotgun would bring them both down.

'Sorry,' Vicky murmured.

Owen forced a thin smile. 'Not your fault.'

'It is. I should never have agreed to have you stay for the week.'

'Wouldn't have missed it for anything,' Owen replied quietly.

She turned back to face her Uncle. 'Liar,' she murmured to Owen.

There was another ear-splitting roar. All of them looked towards the sound. But there was only darkness, broken by the light from the farmhouse windows.

'They're getting very close,' Sergeant Campbell said.

McLaren was standing slightly back from Uncle Andy and Sergeant Campbell so that he could cover the policeman as well as Owen and Vicky with the shotgun.

'What do you want to do with this one?' he asked, jabbing the gun towards Campbell. 'Shall I lock him up with the others?'

Uncle Andy shook his head. 'No, he's too dangerous. And I think we need to teach some of these children a lesson.' He turned to glare at Owen and Vicky before returning his attention to Campbell. 'Kill him.'

'No – you can't!' Vicky shrieked.

'Wait!' Owen shouted.

But McLaren ignored them. He aimed the shotgun at Sergeant Campbell. Owen and Vicky both ran forwards. But they were too far away. They could never reach McLaren before he fired. Uncle Andy was laughing. Campbell looked defiant, unflinching.

The end of the shotgun spat fire, the sound of the blast echoing inside Owen's head.

Campbell took a step backwards. Perhaps it was out of instinct. Perhaps it was out of surprise that he hadn't been hit.

The shot blasted into the empty darkness as McLaren went flying. Ed had rugby-tackled him, crunching his legs out from beneath him just as he'd fired.

Tam and Mikey were running to join him, and soon all three were wrestling with McLaren.

Uncle Andy turned to escape. But Campbell hurled himself at the man, wrapping his arms round him and dragging him to the ground.

'Oh, no you don't!'

Behind them, McLaren pushed Tam away. He wrenched the shotgun away from Ed, butting him in the side of the head with it. Ed recovered and tried to grab the gun, but McLaren fired again – right at him from point-blank range.

Nothing happened. McLaren had already emptied both barrels. Mikey and Ed grabbed the gun and wrestled it away from him. McLaren was fumbling in his pocket as he backed away from them.

'Flare pistol!' Owen realised. He and Vicky ran to help.

McLaren pulled the stubby pistol from his pocket. But before he could bring it up, Owen charged into him. The flare pistol went flying, disappearing into the darkness. Owen tumbled to the ground, the breath knocked out of him.

But McLaren was still standing. He raised a booted foot, ready to bring it down on Owen's head.

Then Vicky hurled herself at the man, knocking him sideways. His foot stamped down, just missing Owen. Catching his breath at last, Owen staggered to his feet.

Campbell held Uncle Andy from behind by the arms. Ed was shaking his head groggily. Nearby, Tam was also recovering. Mikey backed away as McLaren turned towards him.

'How did you get out of the barn?' McLaren snarled.

'Mr Gardner let us out,' Tam told him.

'Though he isn't really Mr Gardner,' Mikey added. 'He's police, so watch it.'

They heard the creature before they saw it. The sound of its roar was so loud that Owen could feel the noise thumping in his chest. Moments later, the monster's savage head loomed out of the darkness, above and behind McLaren.

Mikey dived out of the way. Vicky grabbed hold of Owen, pulling him back. Out of the corner of his eye, Owen saw Uncle Andy tear himself free from Campbell's grip and run off into the darkness, back towards the farmhouse.

But Owen's attention was fixed on the monster as it lunged forwards. McLaren was rooted to the spot, unable to move. His eyes were wide with fear and his whole body was trembling.

The creature tilted its head slightly, looking down at the cowering man. Then, so quickly that none of them had a chance to look away, a huge claw slashed out of the darkness. It caught McLaren across the chest, knocking him to the ground. The massive teeth crunched down on the sprawled figure.

McLaren's cries of fear and pain were lost in the terrible sound of the creature's jaws snapping shut.

Chapter 16

The nearest shelter was the barn. But even as Owen and the others turned to run for it, the wall exploded into fragments. A second monster clawed and tore its way out of the side of the building. Both creatures threw their heads back and roared in unison.

'We have to get to the farmhouse,' Sergeant Campbell yelled. 'Out in the open we have no chance.'

The creatures were already turning towards them.

'They can smell us,' Vicky said.

Together, they raced towards the reassuring lights of the farmhouse. Owen wasn't sure how safe they'd be inside. But, unlike the barn, the building was built of stone and looked fairly solid. If only they could get there …

From behind came the thump of heavy feet as the two creatures stomped rapidly after them. Their roars filled the air.

They reached the house, following the wall, round the corner to the front door. A figure was silhouetted against the light from inside – Uncle Andy.

Closer now, Owen saw that the door was hanging off its hinges. One of the monsters must have been to the farmhouse before scenting them at the barn.

As they approached, gasping for breath, the broken remains of the door were shoved back into place.

'He's shut us out,' Ed shouted.

'We can smash our way in,' Mikey told him.

'Something already did,' Tam said.

The heavy door was cracked and splintered, but still solid. Campbell put his shoulder to it, Ed and Mikey helping. It shifted slightly, but then stopped.

'He's put something against it,' Owen realised. 'Barricaded himself inside.'

'Don't be stupid,' Tam shouted through the door. 'Let us in.'

The reply was muffled, but they all heard what Uncle Andy said: 'No chance!'

'Those things will kill us all,' Vicky screamed at him.

'They'll kill *you*. Which saves me the trouble.'

There was no sign of the creatures yet. Owen could hear them, round the other side of the building. Perhaps they were confused by the smell of the smoke from the chimney. But it wouldn't be long before they found their prey.

'You have to let us in,' Campbell shouted to Uncle Andy, but there was no response. 'Come on,' he said to the others. 'Let's all try.'

They shoved and hammered at the door. It scraped another few centimetres, but not wide enough for any of them to get through. Inside, Uncle Andy was heaving more furniture up against his barricade.

'What about the window?' Vicky asked.

'Too small,' Tam said.

'There's a bigger one,' Owen told them. 'Round the other side.'

'Where those creatures are, waiting for us,' Ed pointed out. His voice was trembling with fear.

'Not any more,' Mikey said quietly. He was looking past Owen, towards the end of the farmhouse.

Everyone turned to see what she was looking at. One of the monsters was standing there, silhouetted against the pale moon. It roared in triumph, jaws dripping. There was an answering roar from the opposite side of the farmhouse.

'Quick,' Campbell urged. 'To the other side. Let's find that window.'

'Let's hope we don't meet the second monster coming that way,' Mikey said.

'And hope that madman hasn't blocked the window,' Tam told him.

Vicky was frowning, puzzled.

'What is it?' Owen asked her as they ran for the end of the farmhouse.

'There were three of those monsters, remember? Where's the third one?'

They reached the back of the farmhouse in time to see the second creature following the first round the far corner. That left the back of the farmhouse clear.

'Bit of luck,' Campbell said.

'Until they work out they can come round different ways and catch us between them in the middle,' Ed told him.

'Which window?' Tam asked.

'The kitchen – at the far end,' Owen said. 'There's an oil tank we can climb up on to reach it.'

On their way along the back wall, they passed a smaller window that looked into the living room. Owen glanced in. Uncle Andy was shoving a desk up against a stack of furniture he had piled up against the door.

As Owen watched, Uncle Andy turned. He wiped his hand across his forehead, breathing heavily from the effort. Then he saw Owen at the window. He walked slowly over, grinning.

'Crazy man,' Tam said, looking in with Owen.

Inside the house, Uncle Andy was still smiling. He drew his finger across his throat in an unmistakable gesture. *You're dead*, it meant.

But then something moved at the back of the room, in the shadows beneath the stairs. It was out of Uncle Andy's line of sight, but Owen could see it. Tam caught her breath and took a step backwards.

Uncle Andy walked slowly over to the window. He made a point of looking at the window, as if gauging its size and working out there was no way anyone could fit through it.

The shadow continued to move, unfolding into a grotesque silhouette. Owen pointed urgently.

'Over there!' he shouted.

But Uncle Andy obviously thought he was telling him to take down the barricade and let them in. He shook his head and wagged his finger.

'What are you lot waiting for?' Campbell asked from behind them.

Vicky, Mikey and Ed were with him.

'Oh no – Uncle Andy!' Vicky leaned past Owen and hammered on the glass.

Inside, Uncle Andy continued to smile and shake his head. But then he caught a movement out of the corner of his eye and turned. The shadow under the stairs reared up to full height, touching the ceiling. Maybe it had been asleep in the warm farmhouse.

'That's why the door was smashed in,' Campbell said.

Uncle Andy backed away from the monster as it took a step towards him. For several seconds he seemed unsure what to do. He looked back at the window – too small for escape. Finally, he ran for the door and started to pull the desk away from the barricade.

Even from the window, Owen could see there wasn't time. The monster was moving. It was hampered by its size in the small room and had to duck under the wooden beams in the ceiling. Its tail sent a table flying. Part of the staircase collapsed as the creature forced its way past.

Uncle Andy gave up the barricade. He edged his way round the room.

'He's making for the kitchen,' Vicky said.

'Good job we didn't climb in there and join him,' Ed said.

The monster charged, smashing through a small armchair as it headed for Uncle Andy. He ran, sprinting across the short space to the kitchen door. He was through, slamming the door shut behind him. But that didn't slow the monster down. It ignored the door and crashed through.

'What now?' Mikey wondered.

In answer, they heard a shout from the end of the farmhouse.

'Help me!'

Uncle Andy was half in and half out of the kitchen window. His hands scrabbled on the top of the oil tank as he tried to drag himself out. The wall above him exploded outwards, stone and brick flying. The monstrous head of the creature smashed through, shaking and roaring in rage.

A massive clawed limb raked down through the air. It slammed into the top of the oil tank with a deep metallic clang. Uncle Andy was almost through the window now.

Almost, but not quite. The creature had his leg. With an immense effort, he pulled it free and crawled across the tank.

'We have to help him,' Vicky pleaded.

'No way,' Ed countered.

But they had no choice now, because the other two monsters reappeared at the end of the house. They were right by the oil tank. One of them pounced. Sharp teeth ripped at Uncle Andy – missing by just a centimetre but tearing into the side of the tank. Dark, viscous liquid bubbled out, pooling on the ground.

The other monster did not miss. Its jaws slammed into Uncle Andy. He screamed. Owen turned away, and Vicky buried her face in his shoulder.

Chapter 17

The world was cast in a pale glow as the moon emerged from behind the clouds. The three creatures were busy with the body at the oil tank. Mercifully, their massive bodies blocked the sight of what they were doing.

'Now is our chance to get away from here,' Sergeant Campbell said.

'They can outrun us,' Ed said. 'What's the point?' He was shivering far more than because of the cold of the night. He pointed towards the monsters. 'We're as dead as *he* is.'

'All they can smell right now is the oil,' Mikey said. 'Trust me, I know how pungent that heating fuel is.'

'So let's leg it while we can,' Owen said.

'Which way?' Vicky asked, pulling away from Owen and wiping her eyes on her sleeve.

'Who cares?' Mikey said.

'Up past the barn will take us towards the harbour,' Tam suggested.

'Good idea. Come on, then.' Sergeant Campbell led them at a jog up the hill.

'This what you expected to find going on here on the island?' Owen asked.

'Far worse. If I'd known the half of it, I'd have made sure the kids' trip was cancelled. Then I'd have brought an armed response team. Maybe the army too.' He glanced at Owen, forcing a weak smile. 'Looks like you guys will have to do instead.'

Just as they reached the top, one of the creatures turned. It sniffed the air, as if catching a new scent. The second creature turned as well. The third was still trying to force its way out of the house though the window. Or, rather, through the hole where the window used to be. The wall was bulging outwards as it pushed through.

'If they come after us, we're done for,' Ed said.

'You always look on the bright side, don't you?' Tam told him. 'You were so hard, the big bully. Now look at you – wimpy kid.'

'Shut up!' Ed shouted at her. 'Just shut up, OK!'

'Oh, well done,' Mikey said.

Below them, the creatures were all looking towards the sound.

'If they didn't smell us, they heard you,' Tam said.

Ed clenched his fists at his side. For a moment, it looked like he was going to go for Tam.

Owen backed away. His foot caught on something in the grass, and he slipped and almost fell. As he staggered back, he saw what he had made him trip.

'Hey – look at this!'

They all turned to see. Ed's hands unclenched.

'What is it?' Campbell asked.

Owen held it up. The stubby gun was heavier than he had expected.

'McLaren's flare pistol,' Vicky realised. 'He drove one of the monsters away with it.'

'Is it loaded?' Sergeant Campbell asked.

Owen had no idea, so he gave it to Campbell. He checked.

'Yes. Just the one flare though.' Campbell looked down to where the two monsters outside the house were walking towards them. They moved slowly as if reluctant to leave their meal. 'One flare won't stop them all.'

'It might,' Mikey said. 'I've got an idea.'

They listened with increasing disbelief as Mikey quickly told them his plan.

'You are kidding,' Tam said when he had finished.

'It's far too dangerous,' Sergeant Campbell agreed.

'And who's going to be daft enough to go back down there?' Ed asked, pointing down towards the farmhouse.

The third monster was still forcing its way through the kitchen wall. It was roaring in frustration, stuck half in and half out of the house. The other two were looking up at Owen and the others. They might attack at any moment.

'Let's face it, we're never getting off this island,' Ed said. 'The boat must have been smashed to bits in the storm. Those monsters will find us. Wherever we go, they'll hunt us down.'

'Oh, grow up,' Vicky snapped.

But Tam shook her head. 'He's right. We don't know when anyone will come looking for us. If anyone ever does. Those things followed us here; they'll keep hunting us unless we stop them somehow.'

'But there must be a less dangerous way,' Owen protested. 'What do you think, Vicky?' He turned, but she wasn't there. She had been right beside him just now – and she had gone.

Owen looked round, puzzled.

'There she is – what's the idiot girl doing?' Ed pointed down towards the monsters.

Vicky was walking slowly and calmly right towards them. As everyone watched in disbelief, her shouts floated back to them.

'Come on, you stupid monsters. Come and get me. You want your dinner? Well, here I am.'

Owen could only watch, horrified, as she approached the monsters. One of the creatures tilted its head to one side, watching her curiously.

'They'll kill her,' Tam said.

'She's cracked,' Ed said. 'She must have a death wish.'

'No,' Owen realised. 'She's doing it – Mikey's plan. She's keeping them near the oil tank.'

'But not too near, not yet,' Campbell agreed. 'Mikey – get down there and do your stuff.'

Mikey swallowed. He looked pale. But he nodded and started running down the hill.

'I'll get closer,' Campbell said. 'The rest of you stay here.'

Owen was watching Vicky as she circled the monsters, drawing their attention away from where Mikey was hurrying down the hill. 'No,' he said. He suddenly felt very calm. 'Vicky needs help.' He ran down to join her.

The two monsters were stalking slowly towards Vicky now. They seemed wary, perhaps confused that their prey was coming to meet them. Owen was out of breath by the time he reached Vicky.

'This is stupid,' he told her.

'So why are you here?'

'Because ...' He sighed. 'Because I'm stupid too, I guess.'

They both backed slowly away as the monsters came closer. At some point Owen and Vicky had started holding hands, but Owen couldn't remember when. Had he taken her hand, or had she taken his? It didn't matter.

'Don't go too far,' Vicky said quietly. 'We need to head back that way in a minute. Is Mikey –'

'He's doing his stuff,' Owen assured her. 'And there's no need to whisper. It's not like those monsters can understand us.'

'You hope.'

Between the two monsters, they could see Mikey at the oil drum. There was a pipe at one side, with a valve attached. Mikey had said it was where the tank was filled from. He was working at it. The valve was close to where the monster had ripped a hole in the tank. Above him, luckily just out of reach, the third creature was still struggling in the wall. It lashed out, trying to reach Mikey.

'He'd better be quick,' Owen said.

The two monsters had raised their heads. One reared up, preparing the charge at Owen and Vicky. At that moment, Mikey turned and gave them a thumbs-up. Then he ran back up the hill.

With a triumphant roar, the third of the creatures finally managed to rip its way through the wall. It emerged on to the top of the oil tank, standing proud and defiant against the moon.

'Now!' Owen yelled.

He and Vicky ran – not away from the savage monsters but straight towards them.

The creatures were taken by surprise. Owen and Vicky managed to dodge past them before they recovered. But as soon as they were past, the monsters turned to follow. Owen and Vicky ran on, holding hands.

Ahead of them, the creature on the oil tank watched through blood-red eyes as they approached. It gathered itself, preparing to leap down and cut them off.

At the last moment, Vicky veered off, pulling Owen with her and heading back up the hill. A short way ahead, Detective Sergeant Campbell stood, the flare gun levelled so it aimed right at them.

'Down!' Campbell shouted.

Owen and Vicky hurled themselves to the muddy ground.

Owen turned to watch as he fell. Behind him, the two pursuing monsters were just passing the oil tank. The third monster still stood on top of it. Dark oil was pouring from the valve on the pipe where Mikey had been working. One of the monsters splashed through the oil as it passed the oil tank.

At exactly that moment, Sergeant Campbell fired. The fiery trail of the flare streaked through the air above Owen and Vicky. It exploded against the side of the oil tank, just above the gushing valve.

For a split second, the flare lit up the side of the farmhouse. Then the oil ignited. The pool the monster was stamping through burst into flame. The monster roared in pain and surprise. But the sound was lost in the colossal sound of the explosion as the whole oil tank blew up.

An orange fireball engulfed the creature standing on the tank. The creature already burning beside it collapsed into the flames. Stone and rubble were blasted across the moorland as the farmhouse wall was blown out by the detonation of the tank.

The last of the monsters was caught full in the blast of rubble. A moment later, another explosion caught the creature. All three were now engulfed in flame and smoke.

The heat of the blast swept over Owen and Vicky as they lay on the ground. The night was alive with orange flame. Black smoke billowed up like storm clouds, blotting out the moon.

Chapter 18

It was snowing again. Large white flakes spun lazily in the air.

'At least it's warm,' Tam said. 'Nice fire, Mikey.'

They sat on the hillside, looking down at the burning remains of the farmhouse. None of the creatures had emerged from the inferno. The smoke made Owen's eyes sting, but he didn't complain.

'A soon as it's light we'll make for the harbour,' Sergeant Campbell said.

Ed sat a short way off, with his knees pulled up to his chin, staring into space. He had said nothing since the explosion. The others had all laughed and jumped up and down, congratulating each other and telling Vicky and Owen how stupid they were. Stupid, but brave.

'So, were you really bluffing and acting on your own, like Uncle Andy said?' Owen asked Sergeant Campbell. 'Or are you here on duty, or whatever?'

'A bit of both,' he admitted. 'My boss agreed there's something weird going on, and he sent me to find out all I could before he took things further. He's been trying to get sense out of the real Mr Gardner.'

'What will the police do now?' Vicky asked.

'Not sure, to be honest. I guess there's your uncle's other business operations that need investigating. He mentioned a team coming in to sort things out – we'd like to talk to them.'

'I bet,' Mikey said. 'Hey, I won't be in trouble again for starting a fire, will I?'

Campbell laughed. 'Not this time. But don't make a habit of it.'

Mikey nodded. 'I've had enough of fires and things getting broken,' he said. 'Things and people.'

'Maybe we won't need to get to the harbour,' Tam said. She stood up, peering into the distance beyond the burning building.

'What is it?' Owen asked.

He could hear the answer as soon as he'd spoken. The rhythmic thump-thump of a helicopter's engine. Moments later, he could see it flying towards them. A powerful searchlight shone down at the ground as it approached.

'They must have seen the explosion from the mainland,' Campbell said.

'All part of the plan,' Mikey told them.

'Liar,' Tam said. She called over to Ed. 'Hey, big fellow – there's a helicopter. We'll be fine now. Come on.'

She jumped up and waved to the approaching helicopter. Soon they were all standing and waving.

Ed pulled himself to his feet and came over to join them. 'Nice one, Mikey,' he said quietly. 'And you guys,' he said to Owen and Vicky. 'Sorry, I guess I'm just tired.'

'We all are,' Campbell said.

The helicopter hovered over them. The searchlight was dazzling. Snow flakes twisted and danced in the brilliant light. Slowly, the helicopter started to descend.

'Sorry,' Vicky shouted above the sound of the engines.

'What about?' Owen yelled back.

'About everything. You had a rubbish time, and then … Uncle Andy and all this.'

Owen shrugged, not sure what to say.

'I won't invite you to my place again,' Vicky promised. 'Recipe for disaster. OK?'

Owen nodded. 'OK,' he told her. 'That's probably best.' Did she look sad at that, or was he imagining it? 'Next time, you can come and stay with me,' he said.

Vicky grinned. 'And no monsters?'

'Just my little brother.' Owen looked back at the burning remains of the farmhouse. 'Those monsters down there are no match for him.'

As the helicopter touched down, the sound of the engines changed pitch slightly, and Owen thought he could hear something else. It was probably just the spinning rotors. But, just for a moment, it had sounded like the distant rumbling roar of some huge creature calling out in the night.

The End

Making Monsters

By Christopher Edge

How to bring a dinosaur back to life

Think the idea of bringing a prehistoric monster back from the grave is science fiction? Think again. In laboratories around the world, scientists are working on research that could turn science fiction into science fact. So what do you need to bring a dinosaur back to life?

Find a piece of amber

Not just any piece of amber though. You need a piece of amber with a prehistoric blood-sucking insect trapped in it. If the insect had sucked up some dinosaur blood before it was trapped, then there might be traces of this blood preserved inside the amber. Because dinosaurs died out over 65 million years ago, this might be the only way we can now get hold of their blood.

A scientist would need to:

- remove the dinosaur blood from the preserved insect
- try to extract the dinosaur's DNA from the blood
- clone the dinosaur using its DNA.

What is amber?

Amber is an orange-yellow substance made from fossilised tree resin. Millions of years ago, any insects landing in the sticky resin would become trapped. Over time, the resin hardened and turned into amber. This means any insects trapped inside are perfectly preserved. Pieces of amber which are over 100 million years old have been found with insects and spiders preserved inside.

What is DNA?

DNA is the blueprint for life. It is found in the cells of every living thing. It contains the instructions that determine how the creature will grow, look and act. If you could find a dinosaur's DNA, then you would have the recipe for bringing it back to life.

Human DNA has been extracted from modern blood-sucking insects, like the mosquito. However, extracting dinosaur DNA from blood found in an insect that is millions of years old is much more difficult!

DNA is delicate and can disintegrate over time. Even if a scientist finds dinosaur blood, they might find that the code for making their dinosaur is incomplete! Where else might they find some dinosaur DNA?

Break a bone or two

Scientists used to think that fossilised dinosaur bones could only show how dinosaur skeletons fit together. However, when the bone of a Tyrannosaurus rex was accidentally broken, the scientists got a big surprise.

Inside the broken bone, scientist Mary Schweitzer found what looked like dinosaur blood cells. These cells survived for 68 million years protected in the fossilised bone. If these blood cells were from a dinosaur, could they contain dinosaur DNA?

At the moment, the technology doesn't exist to extract DNA from these ancient cells. However, in time, could it be possible to clone a dinosaur using ancient DNA?

Some scientists think so and plan to practise their techniques on another extinct prehistoric creature – the woolly mammoth.

Cloning a mammoth

The mammoth, an animal that looked like a hairy elephant, lived over 5,000 years ago. It died out after the end of the last ice age. However, bodies of dead mammoths have been found frozen in the ground in the icy region of Siberia in Russia. These mammoths have been dead for thousands of years, but their bodies have been preserved by the ice.

Using their dead bodies, scientists have been able to discover some of the mammoth's DNA. This DNA shows that the mammoth is very similar to the African elephant, which is still alive today. This has given one scientist an idea about how the mammoth could be brought back to life.

Professor Akira Iritani plans to take a sample of skin or tissue from a frozen mammoth and use this to clone the creature. He will extract mammoth cells from the sample and inject them into the egg of an African elephant. The elephant will then give birth to a baby mammoth!

At the moment, only 30% of attempts to clone animals are successful. However, in 2008 scientists managed to successfully clone a mouse from the cells of another mouse that had been frozen for sixteen years. Professor Iritani predicts that by 2016 a healthy mammoth will be born this way.

If an elephant can give birth to a woolly mammoth, which animal do scientists think could give birth to a dinosaur? You might be surprised by the answer...

Why did the chicken become a dinosaur?

If you look up at the sky, you might spot a distant cousin of the dinosaur. Birds are the closest relatives to dinosaurs living today. Beneath the skin, the skeleton of a bird is similar in many ways to the skeleton of a dinosaur. Scientist Hans Larsson is working on a way to change birds back into dinosaurs.

Larsson is using chicken embryos to do this. In the very early stages before a chicken is born, it has some dinosaur-like features. For example, its tail has sixteen bones in it – like a long dinosaur tail. However, as the embryo develops, these extra bones disappear and the chicken is born with a normal short chicken tail. But Larsson plans to use genetic engineering to bring these dinosaur features back in a live chicken.

So far he has managed to extend the chicken's tail by three extra bones, grow dinosaur-like teeth in a chicken embryo and is now looking into ways to turn the chicken's wing into a dinosaur arm. In time, it might even be possible to hatch a dinosaur!

Next time you take an egg out of the fridge, make sure there's isn't a T-rex lurking inside!

What is an embryo?

An embryo is the name given to an animal at the earliest stage of its development before it is born. In humans, babies are called embryos for the first eight weeks of their life inside the womb.

What is genetic engineering?

Genetic engineering means changing an animal's DNA by artificial methods. A cloned pig with a glow-in-the-dark snout is a famous example of genetic engineering.

We would like to thank the following schools and students for all their help in developing and trialling *Monster Island*.

Royal Manor School, Portland

Adam Clark, Ashley Friend, Karl Jolliffe, Ayrton McCusker, Brandan Plackett, Lawrence Teague-Forder.

Queensbridge School, Birmingham

Farhan Akmal, Farees Almatari, Junaid Asif, Chloe Bartlett, Shane Bevan, Tyler Blair-Thompson, Shahid Farooq, Danial Hussain, Umayr Hussain, Arbaz Mohammed Khan, Kadeem Khan, Umer Khan, Ihtishaam Majid, Arslan Mehmood, Aqila Patterson, Sophie Pinnegar, Aaron Reatus, Jamie-Lee Smith, Roche Smith, Abdallah Suleiman, Imran Uddin, Saqib Ul-Hassan, Chulothe Urooj, Keiran Von-Breen, Nikolas Watkins, Oliver Watkins, Grace Williams, Raakib Zaman.